THE MARSHAL OF
VENGEANCE

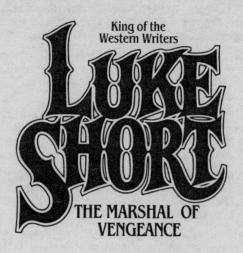

King of the
Western Writers

LUKE SHORT

THE MARSHAL OF VENGEANCE

The Marshal of Vengeance

Under the hard glare of the kerosene lamp, Sheriff Andy Kimber had the look of a small boy accepting punishment for something he hadn't done. There were seven other men there in the office of the Ophir mine. Six of these were managers of mines in the Apache Tanks low grade ore field, and they wore identical expressions as they watched Sheriff Kimber—looks of censure.

The seventh man's lean, weather-browned face was impassive, almost bored. His clothes were those of a puncher, and on his blue shirt was the badge of the town marshal's office. He too was watching Andy Kimber.

Sheriff Kimber squirmed uncomfortably and stroked his longhorn mustache. "There don't appear to be much to say," he allowed. "I just can't fill the job."

"But you know the robber," said Chip Mayhew, manager of the May Star.

"I know *of* him," Kimber corrected. "Cotton Wistrow. Anybody seen him?"

"That's not important. The important thing is to

1

catch him. Any man that can rob five bullion shipments in one month can't be allowed loose."

"I can't do it," Kimber said patiently. "I've tried. Maybe I'm too old. . . ."

"Not even if I tell you that the vice-president of our company wrote me today to close operations unless these holdups are stopped?" Mayhew asked. His square aggressive jaw jutted a little more now.

"Not even then."

Mayhew looked around at the others. "Well?" he inquired. "What do we do now?"

Kimber looked steadily at Mayhew, then at the faces of the other managers. He said, "*I* can't do it, but I think I can tell you a man who can."

"Who's that?" Mayhew asked.

The sheriff jerked his head toward the tall, sleepy-looking young marshal. "Simms Cowan. Three months ago no decent woman dared to walk the streets of Apache Tanks. Today a kid can play in them."

All eyes turned on the young marshal, and he shifted uncomfortably. Simms Cowan was aware that their looks held a certain respect, but no friendliness. He waited, toying with a match.

"I wondered when you'd come to that," a voice drawled. It was Lee Craig, the Ophir manager, speaking. He was past middle age, big, with years of mining experience in the West behind him. Next to Sheriff Kimber, he was the oldest man here, and probably had the wisest head. He shifted his pipe to the other corner of his wide mouth and made no other comment.

It remained for Chip Mayhew to voice the sentiments of the group. "Cowan might swing it," he said slowly. "Only trouble is, I don't know anything about him. Neither do any of the rest of us."

"I'm a marshal," Cowan said slowly. "I don't much like the idea myself."

"No offense meant," Mayhew said.

"None taken," Cowan drawled. "I reckon what you say is true. You don't know much about me."

Kimber lounged off the table and regarded the rest. Well, I've made my suggestion, Mayhew. You've got sixty miles of canyon road between Apache Tanks and the railroad. The man that takes the bullion for these six mines down that road has got to be a scrapper—and a better one than I am."

"We'll talk it over, Andy," Lee Craig drawled. "And I reckon Mayhew'll see it our way. Simms Cowan is the man we need—even if we have only known him three months." He heaved himself to his feet. "If we can agree on that, I don't think this Cotton Wistrow and his men will bushwhack any more of our guards like he did last night. Anyway"—and here he smiled at Cowan—"not if Cowan has anything to say about it."

The meeting broke up. Simms Cowan was the first to leave, unnoticed, silently, as was his way. Out in the night, as he mounted and swung down the road into town, he was smiling. Mayhew was against him, Craig for him, and Craig's word would carry. Once they gave him the job, things would happen in Apache Tanks—but not the things Craig expected.

Apache Tanks was built on the canyon bottom. Ten years ago, when the boom had just come, the buildings along its one long, narrow street had been constructed, and they were of the jigsaw, false-front variety, which solid prosperity had not changed. It had ten fewer saloons than in the boom days, but all were prosperous and orderly, thanks to Simms Cowan. Passing Rogan's keno parlor, Simms pulled over to the hitchrack and leaned down in his saddle, so that he could see the clock through the wide front window. It was five minutes to nine.

He spurred his bay and rode down to the livery stable. At nine sharp, Simms stepped into Rogan's. He looked the place over with one glance and saw that Chip Mayhew was already seated at his customary game of poker. Simms was grimly thankful that Mayhew's habits were so predictable, for Mayhew was at this place at this hour every night in the week. At the bar, Simms ordered a drink and waited, quietly chatting with the bartender.

He heard them come in, and saw them in the bar mirror. They were four rough miners, a little drunk and in a combative mood. They came to the bar and ordered drinks, then one of them apparently noticed Chip Mayhew for the first time.

"Well, well!" he declared loudly. "If it ain't the boss. Gamblin', too."

He started over to the poker game, and the others followed him.

Simms pretended to pay no attention, until the voices raised in a quarrel. Then he walked over to the table.

Mayhew was standing now, an expression of disgust on his face. One of the miners was talking to him.

"I can lick any man at the May Star, Mayhew. I'm tellin' you, tomorrow there won't be a man at work. We're strikin'."

"For what?" Mayhew asked.

"Higher wages."

"The minimum wage in this camp is four dollars a day," Mayhew said drily. "You can live on that and get drunk two nights a week, to boot."

"Who's drunk?" the big miner asked belligerently. He had an ugly look on his broad, stupid face, and his work-soiled clothes and unshaven face gave him an air of tough and stubborn truculence.

"I'd say you were," Mayhew answered bluntly. "Go back and sleep it off. If you have a bone to pick with me, come up to my office tomorrow."

The big miner turned to his friends. "Hear that? We're too drunk to talk to him tonight, he says."

"We ain't too drunk to fight."

"That's an idea," the big man said. He stepped up to Mayhew and swung at his face. Mayhew saw it coming soon enough to block the blow, but it sent him kiting backwards over his chair.

And then Simms Cowan landed squarely in the middle of the fight. He didn't draw his gun. He drove a vicious left into the big miner's face, and even while the man was falling, he waded in. It was the signal for the others to jump him. One leaped on Simm's back, and Simms bent forward, throwing the fellow over his shoulder into one of the other miners. While these two were tangled on the floor, Simms turned his attention to the fourth miner. Fists flailing, he waded in. The fellow tripped over his prone companions, and as he was trying for his balance, Simms lashed out and caught him squarely on the shelf of the jaw. The man fell, tried to rise, couldn't.

The other two were up now, sobered by the sight of two of their number down.

Simms walked up to one, grabbed him by the shirt and said, "Fellow, what'll it be? Are you goin' to walk out of here or are you goin' out on a shutter?''

"I've had enough," the miner murmured.

Simms turned to Mayhew. "You want any charges filed against 'em, Mayhew?''

"I'll leave that up to you," Mayhew said. "You seem to have settled this fight already.''

Simms turned to the miners. "Clear out," he said brusquely. "If you got a kick about your wages, you'll never settle it this way. Go in and see Mayhew tomorrow. But if four of you try and jump him again, I'll let you cool off in the *juzgado*. Now drag it and take them two with you.''

The miners picked up their two companions and carried them out, and Simms turned toward the bar again.

Mayhew was at his elbow. "I was hopin' you'd do that, Cowan," he said.

"Turn 'em loose?''

"Yes. They lead a hard life here. We pay them all we can afford to, what with these holdups, but sometimes it seems as if it isn't enough. And you can't blame a man for working off a grievance when he's had too much to drink. Liquor makes a man say what he thinks.''

"That's about the way I figured it," Simms murmured.

"Well, you saved me a broken jaw. Let's have a drink on it. What do you say?''

Simms accepted. It was when they were finished with their drink that Mayhew said abruptly, "You know, I think I did you an injustice tonight at the meeting. You remember what I said to the others about you?''

"Yeah.''

"I take it back. I'm in favor of hiring you." He looked keenly at Simms. "We don't know much about you here, Cowan. You're a lonesome hombre, but that's all right. If you can handle our business the way you handled these toughs, you ought to be valuable. Maybe it's best we get together after all."

Simms inclined his head. His eyes looked sleepy, uninterested, but his heart was beating excitedly.

"I might as well tell you what we decided after you left. Craig got me in a corner and talked to me. He suggested our six mines pool to pay your wages and the expenses of as many men as you need. In turn, it's your job to see that our bullion gets to the railroad. Fair enough?"

"I reckon," Simms murmured.

"Then I'll tell Craig I've given my consent." He smiled thinly. "You've taken on a real job, my boy." He slapped Simms on the shoulder, said, "Good luck," and went out.

Simms finished his drink. He was wondering if his face showed the elation he felt. The plan had worked. This faked saloon brawl had turned the trick.

Presently Simms left Rogan's. The moment he was out the door, he hurried across the street on the way to his rooms—and he was whistling.

A woman's voice spoke out in the night: "I saw that, Simms."

Simms started, paused. He could see Mary Craig, Lee Craig's daughter, leaning against the dark store front before him. Carefully, he let his face fall into the old mask of carelessness.

"They ought to put curtains in there. I'll tell Rogan," he said.

"You were whistling, Simms," Mary said lightly.

Simms wondered how much she suspected. But as he looked at her, he forgot about his own concerns, for Mary Craig did that to men. She had soft brown hair that Simms longed to touch, and a small pert nose that was dusted with freckles. There was a warm friendliness in her eyes too, and Simms was not unaware that they were especially friendly when he was around. To him, she was a girl in a million, not content to live on the money her father made. She worked. She was human. She was a woman. And still, he let no light of interest creep into his eyes. He motioned now to her books.

"Teachin' at night again?" he asked.

"The German miners. English class," Mary said, watching him. "You didn't answer my question."

"What question?"

"You were whistling, Marshall Stoneface," Mary teased. "Why?"

"Was I?" Simms asked. "I didn't know it."

Mary regarded him curiously. "Was it because you were proud of stopping that fight?"

"Oh, that?" Simms said carelessly. "No, I reckon not. It wasn't anything."

"Simms Cowan!" Mary said impatiently, stamping her foot. "Can't anybody congratulate you without your being surly? I saw that fight. And it was brave."

Simms said nothing, settling into a sullen silence with which Mary was familiar.

"I wonder," Mary said slowly. "You never seem to need help, Simms. And when you help other people, it's just out of a sense of duty. I wonder if some day you won't warm up a little, be human, and forget whatever it is that worries you."

Simms looked up swiftly. "Worries me? What worries me?"

"I wish I knew."

Simms looked at her steadily. "Nothin' worries me, except when folks get curious about me."

Mary's lips parted in surprise. Suddenly she closed them, and her eyes flashed. "I guess I had that coming, Simms—but you're the rudest, surliest man I know! Good night!" She turned and walked up the street, her back straight and proud.

Simms did not smile at her anger. If anything, his face settled into graver lines than usual. Silently he climbed the stairs over Winterhoven's saddle shop. He unlocked the door, struck a match, crossed to the lamp and lighted it.

"Hello, Simms," a voice drawled.

Simms whirled. A man stood with his back to the closed door. He was a puncher in his middle thirties, with a bony, long face and sleepy blue eyes. His hair, under his black Stetson, was dead white. Twin guns were tied down at his hips.

"Hello, Cotton," Simms said evenly. "How'd you get in?"

"The window."

Simms waved Cotton Wistrow to a chair, but stood up himself. He looked at the outlaw without a trace of fear.

"Two men killed in that holdup last night. Still runnin' a shootin' gallery, eh?" he said quietly.

Cotton shrugged. "Why not? Dead men don't talk."

"It never bothers you at night?"

Cotton scowled. "What is this, a camp meetin' or a business deal?"

"Did anyone ever tell you that you ain't much

different from a snarly dog, Cotton?'' Simms drawled.

Cotton's long face got sleepier and more insolent. "Talk away, fellow, and you'll find you've talked yourself into trouble.''

'Not with you, Cotton,'' Simms said. "The only trouble you could make for me is to shoot me in the back. You couldn't do it from the front.''

Cotton straightened up. "Now don't brag,'' he said gently.

"I'm not braggin'. I just want you to know where you stand.'' Simms paused. "You may seem tough to these miners around here and to an old man sheriff, but you're just another hard-case to me, Cotton. Savvy?''

Cotton looked at him bleakly for a long time. Then his face broke into a thin smile. "You're proddy tonight, Simms.''

"I always am when I hear about your bush-whacking.''

"It don't concern you.''

"Not yet. But it will. And when you pull this job for me, it better be the way I want it. No killin'—or I'll hunt you down and cut you to doll rags.''

"All right, all right,'' Cotton said. "Forget it. What's the news?''

"I'm goin' to get the job,'' Simms said quietly. "Now listen to me. I want you to let me through once. The second time, hold me up. The third time, hold me up again. I'll fight. You won't get the bullion, but you'll force me to turn back. After that, you start your raiding. Ride up to ranches and demand grub. Scare woodhaulers, do anything that will let people know you're raidin'. You savvy that?''

"Sure. But what for?''

"Because Craig won't ship any bullion while you're raidin'. It'll keep pilin' up and pilin' up. Then all of a sudden—when I give the word—you quit. Lay low. Craig'll ship." He spread his hands expressively. "And on that raid, we'll clean him out. He'll lose so much he'll have to close down the Ophir, and look for a job."

Cotton smiled thinly. "You're a funny hombre, Cowan. What've you got against Craig?"

"Somethin' you wouldn't understand."

"What?"

Simms looked at Cotton a long time. "He killed my old man," he said quietly.

"How? He's been here fifteen years."

"I know. And fifteen years ago, I was here. So was my old man." Simms walked to the window and stared out into the night. "My old man discovered this Apache Tanks field, Cotton. He staked his claims and blanketed the field. And then the big mines came in. They wouldn't pay dad's price. Instead, they started raidin' him and burnin' him out. Finally, dad had to sell. And he sold to the Ophir." Simms turned and looked at Cotton. "The man that signed the Ophir check was named Craig. I remember that. A year later we moved to Texas, and dad died. He died from the beatin' these Ophir jaspers had given him—on Craig's orders. Now do you see?"

"Then why don't you kill Craig?"

Simms smiled wolfishly. "I'd rather ruin him. Sometimes that hurts worse than a slug in your guts."

Mayhew kept his word. The next night Simms was informed that he could have the deputy's job if he wanted it. He said he'd take it. His work would be confined to guarding bullion shipments. He was supplied with money to hire four good men.

Simms settled down to his new job and worked at it. The third week an attempt was made to hold up a shipment of May Star bullion, but through some quick thinking on Simms' part, the bandits were fought off. Nobody was killed. And, to everyone's amazement, Simms didn't turn back; he took the bullion the remaining forty miles down the canyon, put in on the train and brought back the receipt. Soon the news of his success had spread all over Apache Tanks. But when people congratulated him, Simms kept his mouth shut and looked uncomfortable. Perhaps the reason for this was that he knew he had done nothing, that Cotton Wistrow, following his orders, had let the shipment through.

The next week rumors started coming in. Cotton Wistrow was riding high, wide and handsome again. Because he hadn't made a successful bullion raid for a month, he was turning to raiding the ranches and stealing cattle. Kimber organized a posse and went out to hunt him. The raids stopped. The day Kimber, empty handed, rode into town with the posse, there was news waiting for him that Cotton was raiding again.

Craig called on Simms that night at his rooms.

"What do you think about this raiding?" he asked.

"It's pretty close to the canyon road," Simms said carefully.

"Too close. I've got a shipment ready. Do you think we ought to hold off?"

"I'll take it through," Simms said grimly.

"I don't want to see you walk into real trouble."

"Let me try it."

It was on a Thursday that he left. On Sunday he returned. The old Barlow Sanderson coach he was using was riddled with bullet holes. The four guards were alive, but each of them had a wound. Two of the six horses were dead, two others crippled. Simms' face was powder-grimed and haggard looking. As he rolled the stage up to the Ophir office and climbed off, Craig came running out.

"Did they get anyone?" he asked.

Simms wearily shook his head. "No. But damn them, they tried. They cut down on the lead team and piled the stage up. For two days, forted up behind rocks, we fought 'em. Finally they gave up and rode south. I couldn't take the chance of runnin' into 'em, so I had to turn back. Nothin' else to do."

This was the introduction. For a month the Ophir worked steadily, mining the ore and reducing it to bars, and all the time the bullion shipping was at a standstill. Cotton was raiding with a vengeance, stopping everything on the gulch road. Slowly, steadily, the gold was piling up in the vaults of the mines. Now a new danger occurred to the mine managers; it was conceivable that the mines themselves might be raided. Each day deepened the frown on Craig's face, for the Ophir was the biggest and richest of these mines."

All this time, Simms Cowan complained to the mine managers.

"Why, hell!" he would say, with those eyes of his deep and chill. "I'll take it through. It's got so now we got the choice of bein' robbed on the road or bein' robbed at the mine some night. Give me the word."

But they would not, and Simms was secretly pleased. Then the raiding stopped as abruptly as it

had begun. They waited to see if it would be
resumed, but no word came of Cotton Wistrow.
He was lying low.

It was then that Craig decided to take a chance.
He told Simms that they would try it. All one
night, the bars of Ophir gold were resmelted—and
this time, all the base metal was taken out, and
only the pure gold left. They had accumulated so
that only pure gold could be shipped in one load.

Before daylight next morning Simms and his
four men pulled through Apache Tanks and headed
south along the road toward the railroad. Simms
felt a quiet elation as he sat beside the driver. This
was real money, big money, worth stealing. Its
theft would cripple the Ophir seriously, perhaps
put it out of business. Certainly it would result in
Craig's ruin, would force him to sell out at a
ridiculously low price.

All that day Simms expected the raid.

He wondered how Cotton would arrange it. He
had talked the night before with Cotton Wistrow's
man, who had been loafing around town for a
week. It was settled that the stage would be raided
today.

By afternoon, Simms' nerves were on edge.
Nothing had happened.

"It looks like we'll get by today," the driver
said. "If we make the stage station at the forks,
we'll have better goin' tomorrow."

"We ain't there yet," Simms observed grimly.
Still nothing happened.

Toward dusk they pulled over the lip of the long
ridge. From there, they could see the road winding
down into the valley. At its bottom was a stone

building, the stage station. Smoke was coming from its chimney. Men were out in the yard.

Simms' hopes sank. Evidently Cotton was waiting for tomorrow. As they rumbled down the long grade into the station, he relaxed and rolled a smoke.

"This ain't hardly a place for a woman no more," Simms said.

The stage driver swore with delight. "Son, that place sure looks good to me."

Rolling into the yard of the station, they saw a man out forking hay to some stock in the corral. He waved to them with a friendly greeting. Out on the back porch, a man in an apron waved too, and they yelled at the man on the hay stack. The place had a friendly air.

"Greesham must have changed cooks," said the driver. "He used to have a woman cookin' for him."

The stage rolled to a stop in front of the building. The stage driver stood up and yelled, "All out, you hombres!" to the guards inside. He turned to look at the station and called, "Frank! Frank Greesham!"

The guards piled out and stretched. Simms and the driver climbed down.

Suddenly, seemingly out of nowhere, a dozen men appeared around the corners of the stage station, six at the south corner, six at the north. All had guns out. It was so unexpected that it caught Simms and the guards completely flat-footed.

"Better hoist 'em, gents," a voice said, and Cotton Wistrow stepped out from his men. There was a thin smile on his bony face.

"Welcome, travelers!" he jeered. "We been

waiting for you for quite a stretch. Where you been?''

He was standing in front of Simms now, and Simms mentally cursed him. At least, he wanted the story of the holdup to include that he himself had tried to fight for the gold. This way, he would have to give up without a struggle.

''Yes, it's Cotton Wistrow,'' Cotton announced to the amazed Ophir guards. He turned his head and said to one of his men, ''Take their guns.''

Then Simms acted. Blindly, foolishly, he leaped for Cotton Wistrow, but Cotton wasn't as unwary as he pretended. He dodged deftly, and as Simms lunged, he rapped a gun-barrel across his skull. Simms folded like an empty sack.

Cotton looked down at him. ''Damn fool!'' he grated, and glanced up at the guards. Prudently, their hands were over their heads, ''Take him inside,'' Cotton ordered them. ''And don't make a break when you get in. This place has been taken over by me for the night. Greesham and his cook are tied up, so don't look for help.''

The Ophir guards did as they were bid.

Inside, the bare big room was cluttered with the saddles of the outlaws. Cotton followed them in and ordered them to lay Simms on a worn horse-hair sofa. Then he himself dashed a dipper of water on Simms' face. The outlaws were crowded in behind Cotton now, watching Simms gasp for air and raise himself feebly on one elbow.

''Well, Simms,'' Cotton drawled, ''always want to make it look good, don't you? You're a hero. Didn't you know it?''

Simms glared at him, trying to tell him without

words that he was treading on pretty thin ice. But Cotton only smiled.

"I'm sorry I had to break our agreement, Simms. I couldn't hold you up back yonder, because I thought this was better."

"What are you talkin' about?" Simms asked, menace in his tone.

"Why, don't you remember you arranged to have me hold up the stage and split the loot with you?"

"You got the wrong jasper," Simms said coldly. "Who in the hell are you?"

"Now, Cowan!" Cotton taunted. "Don't crawfish." He turned to the Ophir guards. "Me and Simms arranged for this little holdup, gents. We was to make it a fity-fifty split. Only we ain't any more. I'm takin' the loot and lettin' Craig take care of Simms."

The Ophir guards looked from Cotton to Simms, and then one of them spoke up. "You're wastin' your time, mister. Anybody that knows Simms Cowan would get a laugh out of that."

"Yeah," a second said. "You might as well accuse Craig of robbin' his own bullion."

Cotton frowned. To Simms he said, "Tell them the truth, Simms. We arranged this little party all by ourselves, didn't we?"

"I don't know what you're talkin' about," Simms said, his face cold and contemptuous. But inside him, a deep shame seemed to be crawling through his blood. His own men loyal to the last, would believe nothing bad of him.

Cotton saw how it was going now, and it amused and angered him. He walked over to Simms, who was still resting on one elbow on the sofa.

"You mean to let on you've never seen me before, Simms? You don't know me? You don't know what I'm talkin' about when I say that we framed this holdup between us, and that you told me to keep raidin' until the Ophir gold was piled a mile high?"

Simms smiled thinly. "You've got the wrong party, mister."

Cotton swung on him with the suddenness of a striking snake, and Simms did not have time to cover up. Cotton's fist struck him a glancing blow on the jaw. Simms' head snapped back and he rolled half over. There he lay, limp.

Cotton observed him with smoldering eyes. And Simms, his jaw throbbing with the force of the blow, and his head swimming, heard Cotton say, "That mealy-mouthed tinhorn!"

He heard Cotton's boots scrape on the floor, as if turning around, and he opened his eyes a little. Cotton was standing with his back to him, looking over the Ophir guards and his own men behind them.

"I'll fix him," Cotton said darkly. "Joe, go unload that gold and unhitch. Mickey, go get some grub for us. After we eat, we'll see whether this pious marshal won't—"

Simms exploded into action. He made one swift dive for the gun in Cotton's left holster, whipped it out and up into the outlaw's back. With his other hand he grabbed for the waistband of Cotton's levis, so that the fellow could not wheel away. It was done so quickly, so deftly, that before any of them realized it, Simms had Cotton covered and was using him for a shield. Coming to his feet, Simms palmed out Cotton's other gun and covered the outlaws.

"Unless you shed them guns, hombres, I'm

goin' to blow a hole as big as my fist in this jasper's back. Quick—all of you!''

The guns clattered to the floor. Then Simms said swiftly to the guards, ''Boys, gather up all the guns you can find, then go out and pile in the stage. This shipment is goin' through!''

Under Simms' watchful eye, the outlaws were disarmed. He knew that there were several other men out in the yard and corrals, but he could not take the time to disarm them. Haste was imperative, before one of them looked through a window and saw how affairs were going.

''Cowan, we ain't got a chance,'' one of the Ophir guards blurted out. ''They'll ride us down in three miles.''

''Get on with it!'' Simms said harshly.

When the guns were all taken and the guards were in the stage, waiting for him, Simms started his slow circle to the door, keeping Cotton between Cotton's men and himself. They were watching closely, ready to act if he slipped.

At the door, he jammed the gun in Cotton's back and muttered, ''You're comin' along with me, you double-crossin' coyote! Back out of here, and make it careful. When you get outside, climb up on the top of that stage and lie down.''

Slowly he backed out the door. One of the guards took Cotton then and, while Simms covered the room, Cotton was forced to climb up on top of the stage. Then, as Simms climbed up after him, the outlaws were covered by a guard on the stage.

''Roll her out!'' Simms commanded the driver, and the tired horses were whipped into action. As the stage broke away from the shelter of the stage

station, three men out in the yard looked up, saw
Simms, then pulled their guns and started shooting.
Feet spread out to brace him, Simms emptied both
guns at the trio, and saw one man go down. The
other two ran for shelter.

Cotton, lying flat on the stage top at Simms'
feet, counted those shots. When he had counted
ten, he grabbed Simms' leg and twisted. Together,
on top of that careening, swaying stage, they fell
and grappled. Behind them, they could hear the
first fusillade of the pursuing outlaws.

Cotton had his hands gripped around Simms'
throat. The two men rolled over and over, Simms
slugging desperately to break the hold. Only the
rail atop the stage kept them from rolling off.

The stage was climbing out of the valley now,
thundering along the narrow road, on one side of
which was the canyon.

Simms got a brace for his feet against the rail.
With this leverage, he could put more force into
his blows. Again and again, he drove his fist into
Cotton's face, and finally, when Simms' lungs
seemed about to burst, Cotton's hold was broken.

Struggling to his knees, Simms sucked in his
breath. A few feet away, Cotton was facing him,
an evil grin on his face. "You was braggin' how
tough an hombre you were, Cowan. Let's have a
look!"

For answer, Simms dived at him. Cotton rose to
his feet, Simms following him. Then, toe to toe,
they started slugging, the lurching of the stage
making their blows unsure and wild. Behind Cotton,
Simms could see the first horsemen round the bend
in pursuit. And Simms knew that if they were ever
to escape, he must finish this soon.

Cotton was slugging with wild abandon, crowd-

ing Simms up close to the driver's back, but the
driver could not help. The horses and the narrow,
winding road took all his attention.

Slowly, Simms felt himself being pushed back.
In desperation, he dived at Cotton. They clinched.
Now it was a wrestle; and Simms' broad muscles
sawed and coiled under his shirt as he tried to
maneuver Cotton to a place where he could break
away and smash him hard.

Suddenly Cotton jerked a knee into Simms' groin,
and the swift pain of it was almost nauseating. But
doggedly Simms held on, his hands locked around
Cotton's upper arms. Again, Cotton tried to knee
him, but Simms was too quick this time. He caught
Cotton's leg off the stage top, kicked it sideways.
Cotton lost his balance. And then, with one, sweep-
ing savage blow, Simms laced an uppercut to
Cotton's jaw.

Cotton went back, balanced for one perilous
second on the edge—and a lurch of the coach did
the rest. Cotton sailed clear of the stage top, his
wail of terror keening high in the dusk. The last
Simms saw of him, he was falling over and over in
the air on his way down to the canyon bottom.

Simms did not wait to watch him. He got down on
his belly and stuck his head over the side of the
stage to look inside.

"Give me a rifle and shell belts and a rope!" he
commanded.

They were at the top of the hill now, and the
stage was picking up speed. Behind them, the
outlaws were in close pursuit. He could see the
smoke of their gunfire, but the stage was still out
of range.

The rifle and belts and rope were handed up to

him, and then he crawled up to the stage driver and shouted: "Hunker down in the boot, Abe, and don't stick your head over the stage top. I'll fight 'em off the rear. And drive them horses till they drop. We're takin' this gold through!"

Then he crawled back. With the rope, he fashioned a rough sling, which would hold him no matter how much the stage lurched. Down on his belly, he laid the belts beside him, loaded the rifle and waited.

He did not have long to wait. Soon the outlaws were directly behind the stage and were raining a hail of lead at it. It was so dark now that Simms could barely make out the figures of the horsemen, but he shot at the orange flare of the guns in the dusk. When he was loading up for the second time, he felt a savage blow at his shoulder, and his arm went numb. Doggedly, he managed to load the gun. The orange flares were closer now, and he could hear the yell of the horsemen.

With careful aim, he chose the first orange flare—and fired. There was a sharp yell. When the shots winked again, they were not so close. Simms kept pouring a stream of lead in that direction—and they kept answering.

Darkness settled. It seemed hours that the pursuit continued. The gun-flames would disappear, and Simms would think that the outlaws had given up. Then, a few moments later, the orange powder fire would wink out again, and this time closer than the last. Only the narrowness of the road kept them from being overtaken and the horses shot.

Mile after mile, the running battle continued. Simms' arm felt wet and sticky, and he used it with difficulty. He kept telling himself that he mustn't let any one of the riders pull up even with the stage. If that happened, they would be lost.

Time and again, the outlaws made a desperate bid to overtake the stage; inside, the guards had battered out the back window, and joined in the fight. Simms' rifle was getting so hot that he could scarcely hold it.

It was just breaking day when the stage rolled down to the little railway station and store called Cienega. The stage had not stopped all night. The horses were so weary they could scarcely move. Simms looked back up the grade. There, silhouetted against the graying sky, were five horsemen. He saw their rifles lift to their shoulders, erupt orange flame. It was a hopeless gesture of defiance. The nearly spent slugs rapped harmlessly on the stage top. Then Simms saw the outlaws turn and ride away. The gold was safe.

When the stage pulled up at the depot, Simms wearily saw in the gray light that there were several people waiting there. Untying himself, he found he was so weak that he could not rise. The driver helped him down, and the first man he saw was Lee Craig. Beside him was Mary Craig.

Dazedly, Simms looked at them, wanting to ask how they had got there, but someone took him by the arms and led him in to a seat in the station. Passing the horses, he saw that three of them were foundered, the rest had their heads almost down to the ground.

Inside, someone gave him a drink of water and he took it. Then he noticed that it was girl's hand that had given it to him. Oh, yes, Mary Craig was here. But he was too sick to look at her. He hung his head on his chest while somebody bathed his wound. The pain of it cleared his head a bit, so that he could hear the Ophir guards telling Craig what had happened.

". . . and this Wistrow had the gall to try and claim that him and Simms had arranged for the holdup."

"A coward's way," Lee Craig said contemptuously. "I'm glad I took the shortcut and saw the finish."

Simms raised his head. Through the haze before his eyes, he could see Mary Craig's face. There was concern in it. Simms brushed her aside and tried to talk. At first it wouldn't come, but he persisted.

"It's true," he muttered wearily at Craig. "I did arrange it, Craig."

There was a long silence.

"Were any of my men killed?" Simms asked.

"None," Craig answered.

"Thank God!" Simms put his head in his hand. He knew they were waiting for him to explain. Finally, when he had the strength, he said, "I've hated you, Craig. I wanted to ruin you. I fixed it up with Cotton Wistrow to keep raiding the canyon, so your gold would pile up. And when you got enough of it, we planned to rob you."

"I don't believe it!" Mary said staunchly. "You're out of your head, Simms."

Simms looked up now, and in his weary eyes was the old look of hardness.

"No, I'm not. I wanted to ruin you, Craig."

Resentment glowed in Simms' eyes as he looked squarely at Craig. "My name isn't Cowan. It's Combs—Bill Combs. Your Ophir outfit stole that gold field from my father, Dave Combs. You swindled him and ruined him, and he died of it. And there was a man by the name of Craig, I remember, who worked for the Ophir.'' He paused and said quietly, ''That's why I hate you, Craig. I just wanted to even an old score.''

''And why didn't you?'' Craig murmured softly, his eyes kind and gentle.

Simms looked down at his hands. ''I found that my men believed in me. I had to be honest. It's—it's somethin' I couldn't dodge, Craig. I'd tolled them in to their deaths, and I couldn't leave them.'' He looked at Craig. ''Damn you, I'll get even! If I can ever hold a gun again . . .''

Craig shook his head. ''Son, let me tell you a story. That Craig you remember was a scoundrel—the blackest scoundrel that ever lived—and my brother. When he was killed, I inherited the mine. It was only two years ago that I learned the whole story of how my brother got it. Since then, I've been hunting the whole West for a man by the name of Bill Combs. I wanted to settle with him for the injustice that had been done him. All the gold that's been taken out of the Ophir is waiting for him. I've kept only a superintendent's wages.'' He paused. ''Do you still want to kill me, Bill Combs?''

Simms was too weary to understand this immediately, but as it sifted through his weary consciousness he looked at the floor. After a long time, he raised his head.

''I'm sorry, Craig. I . . . My God, what did I almost do?''

He put his face in his hand. Minutes later, he felt a hand on his head and he looked up. It was Mary.

"Old Stoneface," she murmured. "Not so tough as you wanted to be."

Simms smiled crookedly and took her hand, but he could not speak.

"I'll say it," Mary said softly, kneeling before him. "I've seen it, Simms. I've wanted to make you speak out. You love me, don't you?"

"I always have," Simms murmured. "But dad came first."

"And I love you," Mary said. "There, that wasn't hard, was it, Simms?"

"Combs is the name, Mary." Simms was smiling.

"Mrs. Combs is the name, Bill," Mary said. "Or it will be—I hope!"

And Simms kissed her.

The Ghost Deputy
of Doubletree

The shiny new badge in Wes McGrew's pants pocket was ramming into his leg, and he shifted his position ever so faintly, a look of weary disgust stamped on his face. He had been here since noon, flat on his belly in the mesquite of the rimrock, a carbine by his side.

It was almost dusk now, and below him on the canyon floor, the brush corral that lay by the spring was in deep shadow. Around him was the silence of the desert.

"Three hours of sandflies and no smokes," he thought savagely. "All because Reardon had a half-hearted tip that the Circle R stuff pushed out of them Lost River brakes last night would be watered here. Hell!" He cursed with the passion only a new deputy balked on his first job could muster, and then settled down again to a simmering silence.

But not for long. The sound that yanked him to attention was a strange one. It was a gibberish shouting, made by a man who was lost to sight around the bend of the canyon below. Wes wormed his way through the brush until he had a clear view of the spring, pulled his carbine up beside him and laid his cheek on the stock, waiting.

In another minute, two small calves trotted into view, paused alertly, sniffing, then scampered playfully up to the spring and began to drink. Following them was a man on foot, but such a man that Wes did not even bother to raise his rifle.

The man was raggedly attired in an old black suit, a battered felt hat and heavy, rocking-chair brogans. He removed his hat when he reached the spring, tucked a stick under his arm and, pulling a bandana from his pocket, mopped his face while looking around at the cliffs above him. He was a Chinaman.

Wes, mouth hard, rose cursing, crashed out of the brush and picked his way down the canyon-side.

Walking up to the man, Wes demanded, "Who the hell are you?"

"Sam Sing. Velly hot, velly tired, velly sore as hell."

Wes indicated the two calves. "Where'd you get them? Where you goin'?"

"Me cook for 7L over mountains. On way to new job for Box K. I lide mule shortcut when big fellas all same stop me and take mule."

"Wait a minute," Wes cut in. "What big fellas?"

"Four," Sam Sing said, and shrugged. "Him dlive lotsa cattles. Him take my mule. Him pull two calves from big bunch and tell me to come here."

"Here?" Wes echoed slowly. His mouth closed, his jaw muscles bulging. All the slackness that had been in his body left, and he straightened, his blue eyes chilling a little. Lean, of medium height, inclined to slimness, his gathering anger seemed to make him tower above Sam Sing. "Tell it slow," he drawled. "You met four jaspers drivin' a herd of beef. They stopped you, took your mule and told you to drive them over to this spring. When was that?"

"Sun-up."

"Did they tell you I'd meet you here?"

"Him say man wait for me, give me baby cows."

"He did, did he?" Wes said truculently. "What else did he say?"

"Him say nice depitty fella with fine badge here to meet me, and him give cows to me and lide me to Doubletlee." He paused, smiling with a mouthful of bright teeth and an expression that beamed friendliness.

Wes cuffed his Stetson back on his head and put hands on hips, his mouth open to question, argue and curse his hard luck, when he checked himself. Suddenly, he grinned, and Sam Sing grinned back at him.

It was useless to tell Sam Sing what had happened, that he had met the rustlers whom Sheriff Reardon had sent one lone deputy to arrest, and that these rustlers, certain that Wes would be waiting here, had played this sardonic and arrogant joke on him. Wes thought savagely of how he would look riding back into Doubletree. He had gone out armed to the teeth on a foolhardy errand; he would return with a Chinese cook mounted behind him; hazing two trail-weary calves ahead of him. And the whole town of Doubletree, long ago convinced that Sheriff Reardon and anyone connected with his office were jokes, would laugh long and loud.

Wes didn't mind the town laughing. They had

laughed when kindly old Reardon had hired him, and they would continue to laugh until he had proved himself. But he did mind the other deputy, Barney Lothar, laughing. Lothar had picked up the tip that the rustlers would water here, in the Lady Gay saloon and had relayed it to Sheriff Reardon last night for what it was worth.

"Personally," Barney had said to the sheriff, his dark eyes mocking, "I think it's a phony. As long as they know we're at the spring, they'll figure we can't be anywhere else."

Wes put in, "But it's the only water close to a straight trail out of the county."

"Listen, Bud," Barney had said tolerantly, "when you've traveled this county like I have, you'll know better. I can find you six dry stream beds over west that haven't run water for months. But you can dig down a foot in the sand with a short-handled shovel and you'll have enough water for a hundred head of stock."

"Then why don't we go to them places?" Wes had asked doggedly.

"There's three of us. There's at least six of them water holes. We can't be in two places at once. And if we deputize enough men to cover it all, the news'll be to the rustlers before we can move. They'll move north in the brakes, risk a dry drive and shake us. They can drive out of those brakes north without leavin' signs."

"That's what they'll do," Reardon put in gently.

Wes said, "I'd like to go over to that Snake Creek spring all the same."

"Go ahead," Reardon said. "It'll show we done something."

"Something damn foolish," Barney said drily. "But let the younker do it. He ain't done anything to earn a feed yet. If he brings back the herd, I'll buy it and eat it at one sittin'.''

So now Barney had been proved right. Wes said to Sam Sing, "Stay here. I'll get my horse. I'll take you back to town—dammit!"

Once Sam Sing was mounted behind him and the calves were moving on ahead, Wes fell to musing. Someone had told the rustlers that he would be waiting here, and nobody knew for certain—except Barney and Reardon and himself— that he would be here. Then how was it that the rustlers had told Sam Sing a deputy with a nice shiny badge would be waiting for him? There was a leak somewhere, and Wes knew it was bound to have come from the sheriff's office. He smiled grimly and let his horse have its head. They'd laugh. Lucy Freeling would hear about it and she wouldn't laugh, but she'd pity him, which he hated more. And the more level-headed men of the town would say, "Ever since Charley McGrew died, Wes McGrew is tryin' to fill his old man's pants. But hell, he'll never make the lawman his old man was. Look at him." And if possible, Wes hated that more than he hated Lucy's pity.

As he expected, the boys were lined up on the Lady Gay's wooden-awninged porch when he came into town that night. The light cast out in the street by the stores fronting the single thoroughfare of shadeless and sun-baked Doubletree lighted his entrance to town as though he were a medicine show. He heard the laughter just as he breasted the Lady Gay.

"Gawd, I never thought them rustlers got away with that much Circle R stuff," a voice drawled in mock awe. A shout of laughter followed.

"Who's that tough hombre behind him? The leader?" another asked.

"Why, man, can't you tell?" a third voice answered. "That hombre's from the hard forks of Bitter Creek. I'm goin' in and pull the shutters and lie down on the floor till he's blowed town."

That last was the voice of Barney Lothar. Flushing, Wes glanced over at the Lady Gay's porch. Lothar was leaning against a post, thumbs hooked in belt, his burly body shaking with laughter.

Sam Sing murmured, "Plenty funny, huh? Like hell!"

Barney's voice cut through the laughter again. "And look at that lawman. The famous deputy of Pipestone County. Couldn't track a Conestoga wagon across a field of daisies."

That last remark was the final straw for Wes. He reined in, swung out of the saddle and walked stiff-legged over to where Barney Lothar was waiting. Silence fell among the watchers.

Wes said thickly, "Maybe I ain't such a git-down, hell-fire deputy, Barney, but I reckon I'm the only thing that'll past for one in our sheriff's office."

Barney's taunting grin faded a little. "You been talkin' to your girl."

"Mebbeso I have. But the point is, I ain't been talkin' to a bunch of the boys in the Lady Gay while someone else does my work."

Barney gestured to Sam Sing still seated behind the saddle of Wes's horse. "You call that work?"

"I know where the herd passed. Tracks ain't hard to read. If I'd had another man with me, we'd be on their trail right now," Wes drawled quietly.

"*Another* man?" Barney echoed derisively. "Hell, I ain't seen *one* yet."

Wes's hand reached down and unbuckled his shell belt; it slid to the dirt at his feet. "That'll cost you about four of them nice shiny teeth, Barney," he said thickly. "Will you step off that porch, or do I have to drag you off?"

Barney looked over the crowd lazily. "What's the fine here for smackin' down a fresh kid?" he asked.

Wes took one quick step forward, reached up, twisted Barney's shirt-front in his fist and yanked. Barney, unprepared, came off the porch like a sack of meal, but before he had landed on the sidewalk, Wes had swung, and the blow caught Barney flush in the mouth, catapulting him back so that he tripped on the porch and sprawled on his back.

Barney rose groggily, spitting teeth. With a growl in his throat he took two running steps and leaped off the porch at Wes.

Seeing him coming, Wes stepped quickly aside, and as Barney lit, he swung again, this time at the ear. Again Barney sprawled, and once more he was up. By now Wes knew he was in for a murderous fight. If Barney, fifty pounds heavier and four inches taller, ever got hold of him, Wes knew he was gone. But he didn't care. Barney was slower, and Wes relied on that one fact. Before Barney could get going, Wes sailed in, his fists flailing, arms pumping like pistons. A hot, red rage had come over him. All he cared about was tearing Barney Lothar to pieces.

His first five blows drove viciously into Barney's unprotected face, and after that the fight was as good as over. Barney was stunned; only a dogged instinct of will kept him fighting. But each blow he landed on Wes was bone-crushing.

Wes dodged most of them. He could see that Barney was hurt and hurt bad. He maneuvered around until the light from the Lady Gay was full on Barney's face, and then he waited for one of Barney's dogged and senseless rushes.

It came, with Barney's arms reaching out to grab Wes. Wes stood still, taunting him, baiting him. When Barney's fingers touched his shirt, he started one from the ground. He put everything he had in it, all the hate and strength and disgust and weariness that had been balled up within him for weeks. The impact of it was terrific.

Barney dropped to his knees and rolled in the dust at Wes's feet. He lay there motionless, unconscious. His chest heaving with the effort to get his breath, Wes turned around to the crowd.

"Any more of you jaspers think along with Barney?"

But Wes had won the crowd as well as the fight. A man spoke up and said, "Hell, kid, we was only hoorawin' you. Me, I'm glad you combed him over."

A murmur of assent rose from the rest, but Wes was in no mood to accept it. "You better take him down to the office," he said shortly. "I reckon Reardon'll want to know what happened to him."

Still raging inside, he walked over to his horse, took the reins and led him down the street, hazing the calves ahead of him. Once his horse was grained and watered and corraled, along with the calves, he flipped Sam Sing a dollar for the night's lodging and headed down street for the sheriff's office, which was situated on the lone four corners of Doubletree.

Wes could almost see Sheriff Andy Reardon, with his look of bewilderment and mild exasperation, but instead of dreading the meeting, as he ordinarily would have done, tonight he would welcome it. For his disgust now included even Andy Reardon, who had given him his deputy's job and his father his before him. For the first time, Wes began to understand the vast and farcical incompetence of the sheriff and his office, an incompetence which cattle thieves could mock at, at their will, and which allowed deputies to brawl on saloon porches.

Wes walked into the office with a swagger. Before the cot on which Barney Lothar sat wiping the blood from his face, stood Sheriff Reardon, a slack, untidy figure far into old age. On his amiable features was a fretted look, in his rheumy eyes, one of reproof.

Wes decided to beat him to it. "All right, Sheriff. I done it I'll do it again—just so long as that Big Wind talks out of turn."

The sheriff shook his head. "Deputies fightin' in the streets. What's become of this office anyhow?"

"You tell me," Wes snapped back. "Or, if you like, I'll tell you. It's just this. Not a man here, besides me, gives a damn about law in this county. You won't, I can't alone, and Barney's just too damned lazy."

Instead of flaring up, the sheriff sighed. "I'm old, son. Besides, I never was really a lawman, even if I have been voted into the job ten times."

Wes suddenly felt ashamed of himself. The sagging jowls, the peering and faded blue eyes, the dragging movements of Sheriff Reardon, all attested to the truth of what the lawman had just said.

Reardon, sitting down, added wearily, "There was a time when I could hire deputies to do what was to be done for me. Now, it seems I can't."

Wes looked at Lothar, who was glaring at him, then he said to Reardon, "Give me a man who'll work with me and I'll do it."

Lothar laughed unpleasantly, and Reardon said, "But you're the junior deputy, son. I can't give you a hand over Barney."

"I just took it," Wes said grimly.

"That was luck," Barney growled. "You'll never do it again. You caught me off my guard, or it'd never of happened."

"You want to try your luck again then?" Wes asked truculently.

"Here! here!" Reardon snorted. "No more of that. It's bad enough it had to happen once, without you goin' into it again."

Barney's face was ugly now. His voice was thick. "I'll tell you one thing, Runt. There won't be any more sluggin' matches between us. The next time you feel froggy, just remember you carry an iron!"

Amazed, Reardon got to his feet and walked between them. He put his hands on Wes's shoulders and forced him into a chair, then he addressed them both.

"This can't go on," he said gravely. "Why—"

"Can't it?" Barney sneered. He stood up now, facing Reardon. "Try and fire me, Reardon. You forget my brother's a director in the bank. Maybe you've forgotten too that the bank holds a few pieces of paper on your spread. Fire me, and maybe I'll help put those two and two together.

Then you'll be in shape to serve eviction papers on yourself.'' He laughed quietly, through puffed lips, then strode past the sheriff. He paused at the door, looking at Wes.

"Maybe you noticed I didn't mention anything to Reardon about you goin' or stayin','' Barney said. "I don't care much, one way or the other, because I figure I can take care of you just as easy as I can take care of tomorrow's breakfast. Only—'' he paused and said slowly—"don't forget what I said.''

And with that he stepped out.

Before Wes left the office he told Reardon the plain facts concerning his experience with the rustlers that afternoon. So preoccupied was Reardon that he did not think it strange the rustlers should know about Wes's presence there, and Wes did nothing to enlighten him. He left Reardon slumped in his chair, a worried and helpless old man.

Outside, ravenously hungry, Wes turned up the street to the O. K. Cafe, which Lucy Freeling owned and ran. She had just served a puncher at the counter as Wes entered, and the look she gave him, the cheerful smile on her bright clean face, somehow made up for the disappointing day. Wes sat down and watched her attend the puncher. Her hair was ash blonde, as light as his own was dark, but Wes did not share the calm serenity in her face.

She came over to him in a moment and, smiling, said, "You don't like being teased, do you, Wes?''

Wes flushed. "Not by some people.''

"What happened? I saw the fight-part of it.''

Wes told her all of it, from riding out to Snake Springs to what the sheriff had said. When he was finished, Lucy said, "You're going to stick at it,

Wes? Even in the face of the sheriff's indifference and Barney's threat?''

Wes nodded calmly. "I got a job set me is all. Either I'm a deputy and will swing it, or else I ain't and I'll lay down on it. I—"

He looked over at the puncher, a man he did not know, and he wondered if he should talk. But the puncher saved him the trouble of deciding, for he got up, paid his check, tipped his hat to Lucy and went out.

Lucy came back and said to Wes, "Let me take this stuff out to the kitchen and then we can talk." She went over to the puncher's place and picked up the dirty dishes. As she lifted the plate, she saw a piece of paper under it. Slowly, she set the dishes down and picked up the paper. Then she looked at Wes. "It's for you."

Wes took the paper. It was one of the restaurant napkins and on it was printed in pencil:

McGrew,
    Yore spelled down. Turn in yore badge and you'll live longer. Dont and see what happens. theres a sugar bowl in front of you. if you want to quit, put bowl at the end of the cownter next to the windo. if you dont, then its yore hard luck.

The note was unsigned. Wes read it and looked out the broad window into the dark street. He could see nothing, but he felt he was being watched.

Lucy, her eyes on him, said, "Careful, Wes."

"Careful, hell," Wes murmured.

He walked to the door, opened it and stood in it for a long moment. Most of the stores had closed, so that the street was almost in full darkness. Only across and down the street were there any lights. The hitchracks were almost empty. No one was on the far sidewalk. Still Wes had the feeling that he was being watched. He stepped back into the cafe.

"You go back near the kitchen door, Lucy," he said grimly.

She obeyed. Then Wes looked at the counter. There were five sugar bowls on it, and lest his move should be misinterpreted, he gathered them all up and put them at the far end of the counter toward the kitchen, as far from the window as he could. Then he turned and started for the door again. Gunflame, spearing through the darkness at him, stopped him dead.

The kerosene lamp overhead blinked out, went smashing to the floor on the heel of the load of buckshot which whupped into the wall. Lucy gave a sharp cry, and Wes stooped down, running for the door. Another shot ripped out, and this time Wes saw it was from the roof of the store across the street. He palmed up both guns now and opened fire through the shattered window. Shots answered him.

Careless of what might happen, he plunged through the doorway out into the street, dodged under the hitchrack, crossed the street and knifed in between two store buildings. Pausing behind the store, he listened for footsteps, but all he could hear was the commotion swelling now in front of the Lady Gay. As his eyes accustomed themselves to the dark, he could make out a ladder stretched up to the roof of the building from which the bushwhacker had shot.

He climbed it quickly. Halfway across the flat roof, he could see the prone form of a man. Without moving, Wes observed it a moment, and then he did a strange thing. He turned to the ladder, lifted it, and moved it down six feet toward the front of the building. Below him, he could hear the excited shouts of the men on the street, and he hailed them. In another moment, led by Loosh Moley, of the Circle R ranch, they swarmed up onto the roof.

Wes, kneeling by the figure, said, "Here he is."

Barney Lothar approached with Moley, a gray, grizzled rancher who had been harried these past months by the cattle thieves.

Barney said, "You touched him?"

"Look at the blood," Wes said curtly. "I waited for witnesses."

Now that there were men around, he turned the down man over. He was dead, certainly, shot in the neck. No one knew him, nor could they remember having seen him before.

"What happened?" Moley asked, and Wes told them, not mentioning the note that he had found written on the napkin in the restaurant. Moley scowled, "Search the body," he said. "Maybe he's got somethin' in his pockets that'll give us a clue."

It was Barney who kneeled down to search. The bushwhacker's levi pockets revealed coins, dirty matches, chewing tobacco—nothing else.

"Look in his shirt," Moley said.

Barney pulled out a tobacco sack and some folded papers. The freshest looking one, he opened, and by the light of a match, read it. Then silently he handed it to Moley to read. Wes looked over Moley's shoulder and saw that the paper was a check for five hundred dollars drawn on a Tucson bank. It was made out to Will Armbruster. And the signature it held was that of Andy Reardon, the sheriff!

Moley looked around at the ring of men. "This is a check made out to this bushwhacker and signed by Andy Reardon," he announced calmly. "I reckon it was to pay for young McGrew's beefin'."

Barney Lothar rose. "I don't believe it," he announced flatly, through puffed lips.

"I don't either," Wes said, just as flatly.

Moley smiled meagerly. "I might expect that from you, Barney. But hardly from you, Wes."

"Reardon wouldn't do a thing like that," Wes said. "You can say anything about him you want, but no one could claim he'd ever pay one man to beef another."

Barney looked over at Wes. "Wait a minute," he drawled. "That check could have been planted on this ranny."

Wes said quietly, "Meanin' I planted it, Barney?"

"Maybe that is what I mean!"

Wes's hand dropped to his gun, but Moley, stepping in, clasped his wrist in a grip of iron.

"Easy, son," he said quietly, and turned to Barney. "Lothar, your talk'll get you in trouble yet, real trouble. Watch your mouth!"

"I'll watch it," Barney said, glaring at Wes. "But damn if I believe Reardon would do this. I can't see any other explanation for it, except that the note was planted on this ranny! Someone had to do it. Wes McGrew was the only one around, and he wants Reardon out."

Wes said quietly, "Barney, you and me are goin' to have a little powwow someday—someday soon. And it'll end with one of us goin' out on a shutter.''

"That's enough," Moley said. "Damned if I see what you're rowin' about. You both claim Reardon never done it." Again he looked around at the group of watching townsmen and said, "Me, I think he did."

A murmur of assent rose from the men around him. Wes listened in silence as Moley went on, "This sheriff's office has been kicked around between kids and old men long enough. I dunno why Reardon would want McGrew dead. Maybe McGrew understands why and where all this rustled beef goes. Enough fightin' between lawmen in this town has gone on tonight for a man to expect anything." He turned to Wes. "Did you row with Reardon tonight?"

"We all rowed," Barney put in surlily.

"Then I'm goin' down and talk to Reardon," Moley said. "You deputies keep away."

"Not me," Barney cut in stubbornly. "Reardon is bein' saddled with somethin' and I aim to hear it."

Moley frowned. "All right. So long as McGrew doesn't come too. I want Reardon's story straight. Wes, you stay clear."

Wes nodded slowly, puzzled. The dead man was picked up and lifted down to men waiting on the ground, and Moley, Barney still by his side, left the roof with the others. Wes watched them go, standing motionless, his mind confused.

Reardon was being accused of paying to have him beefed! It was impossible, yet the signature on the check was genuine enough. And Barney Lothar, who had contemptuously threatened Reardon this same night, was now defending him, and doing it violently! It didn't make sense.

Wes shook his head and came back to his first hunch, the hunch he had had when he first climbed up on the roof. It was a simple one. He knew that his shots from Lucy's restaurant below couldn't have hit this bushwhacker where he lay. And that argued that someone else had killed him. Whoever it was would have had to be up here on the roof. He was sure of that, for he had heard both rifle and shotgun shots from the roof.

Wes felt in his pockets and found he had many matches. Then he started a patient search of the roof. Immediately, he was rewarded. There were several cigarette butts against the false front, which argued that the bushwhackers had been waiting there for some time. But more than that, examination showed that there were two kinds of cigarette butts, those rolled with brown paper and those rolled with white. Wes knew enough about punchers to know that every man has a preference, and that he will smoke all brown papers, or all white, never both unless he has to. Here was proof then that there were two men sent up to ambush him. They had tried to, and failing that, one had cut down on the other, planted this check in his shirt pocket, and then ran. That much was certain.

Wes walked back to the ladder and climbed down it. Once on the ground, he moved over to where the ladder had originally been placed. His idea in moving it had been only caution; he did not want the tracks tromped out by the townsmen swarming around it.

Striking a match, he examined the ground at the base of where the ladder had stood. He found one set of tracks which he matched with his own and found were his. These eliminated, he sought others. Then he saw two together, some four feet away from the ladder, the heels of the tracks deep in the dirt, indicating that halfway down the ladder, someone had jumped, then run.

These were the tracks of the man who had shot at him, who had killed his own ally, planted the phony check and run.

Satisfied, Wes made his way to the street. Lucy was waiting across the way, and he waved to her and headed for the sheriff's office.

At the office he found Andy Reardon ringed by a circle of men, of whom Moley was the leader. Beside Moley stood Barney Lothar, and Barney's brother, Max. Wes smiled wryly. Max Lothar was as big as Barney, but he was better fed, gone to slack, and his appearance suggested that he thought his expensive clothes might make up for his big belly, his soft hands and his florid face.

Reardon caught sight of Wes and his eyes were imploring. "Wes, you don't think I done this to you, do you?"

"I never thought so, Andy," Wes said.

Max Lothar snorted. "When it comes to the place where a sheriff tries to kill off his own deputy, somethin' ought to be done about it," he growled. "We've stood for rustlin' and town brawlin' and stage robberies and other things from you, Andy, but I reckon this is the last straw."

"But I—"

"You can't dodge this, Andy," Moley said, holding out the check. "Ain't that your signature?"

"It looks like it," the lawman admitted.

"And didn't you write the check?"

"I swear I didn't."

Max Lothar said, "And I don't suppose you know this Armbruster, the gent on whom we found this check?"

"I swear I never saw him in my life," Reardon said plaintively.

Barney put in, "You're wrong, Max. And you, too, Moley. I've worked with Reardon and I know him better than any of you. This is a frame-up. I dunno whose, but it is. And Reardon is as innocent as any man in the room."

Wes elbowed his way to Moley. "What's this all about, Loosh? I'm the one that was shot at. If there's any complaint sworn out, then I'm the man to swear it. And I'm damned if I will. So go home, the whole lot of you."

Moley looked from Wes to Barney and then back to Wes. "How bad do you two gents want your jobs?" he asked flatly. "I'm head of the county commissioners here and I can call a meetin' in damn short order. If I do, that meetin' will ask for two resignations—as well as the jailin' of a sheriff that tries to beef his own deputy. What about it?

Confronted with this, Wes had no answer. He wanted more than anything in the world to keep his job until he had proved himself. His protest against the arrest of Reardon would get him nowhere. Moley and the commissioners would force Andy Reardon to dismiss his two deputies, and hire two more who would follow the commissioners' orders. Max Lothar, with the paper he held on Reardon's spread, would put on the pressure and Reardon, weak at all times, would submit. No, there was no use fighting it.

He shrugged. "No call to get het up about it, Moley. I'm only doin' what I think is right. I got no complaint against Andy. But if you think you have, then lodge it.''

''I am,'' Moley said flatly, turning to Barney. ''I'm lodgin' it with the senior deputy in the name of the county commissioners. I say for him to arrest Andy Reardon and lock him up until this thing is cleared up once and for all. And by that time, I aim to have a new sheriff up and an election called.''

Barney glared at him. ''Okay, Loosh. You're makin' a mistake, but I can't help it.'' And with that, the gathering broke up.

Next morning when Wes had breakfast at Lucy's, he told her about the happenings of the night before.

''And you're still going to stick it out, Wes? Knowing that you'll have to take Barney's orders?''

''He wants to clear Reardon as much as I do,'' Wes told her. ''Besides, I owe it to Reardon. He gave me my job.''

Lucy said nothing, and Wes left and went down to the office. Barney was already there.

He nodded to Wes and swung around in the swivel chair. ''Kid, we don't see alike on many things, but I reckon we do where Reardon's concerned. It's a dirty frame-up. We're out to get the jaspers that framed him.''

''So you don't think it was me?'' Wes said.

Barney smiled through cut lips. ''No, I reckon I lost my head last night. I never thought much of you, and I do of Reardon. Last night, it come out. But when I stopped to figure it out, I reckon I sounded mighty foolish. There's no sense in your framin' Reardon that way. Where would it get you? Besides, I think you like Andy as well as I do."

"Better, I'll bet," Wes thought, but he only said, "Well, how you aim to begin?"

Barney scowled. "It looks like we ought to begin by checkin' up on the strangers around here, to see where this Armbruster come from. You can bet he didn't try to gulch you just because he didn't like your looks. Somebody paid him, and it wasn't Reardon. If we can find where he come from, what he did and who his friends was, we may get to the man."

"Who'd want to get me out of the way except those rannies that stole the Circle R beef?" Wes asked.

"Mebbyso. Let's find out who they are."

"How?"

"By findin' out where Armbruster come from. He's likely tied up with the same gang."

"And how do you aim to find out?"

Barney scowled. "You know that surly devil, Jud Benson, over east near the line? Well, he don't have many cattle and what he does have wouldn't give work to three hands. Yet he pays six men and they never stay more than a month at a stretch. Do you reckon he might be firin' all those men just as a blind, so's he could hire more? Them he fires might be driftin' over to that gang in the brakes. Jud might be the recruitin' agent."

"He might," Wes conceded. "I doubt it though. He's just plumb tight and mean. Men won't work for him."

"All the same though, we ought to check up on it. And that's your job, McGrew. I want you to ride over there today. Put up with him tonight, talk to his men, keep your eyes open. See if they look

like hard cases. Find out if Armbruster worked for
him. Find out anything you can.''

Wes shrugged and rose. "*Bueno*. We'll at least
be doin' somethin' anyway.''

Wes got his horse, saddled up and rode out east
toward Jud Benson's place. He had many long
hours to review everything that happened yesterday,
and he did; but when he was finished, he was just
where he had begun. He was sure of only one
thing—Barney Lothar was a man to be watched.

The road out to Jud Benson's skirted the Lost
River brakes for several miles, then dived into
them, crossed the river, and climbed out into the
canyon-shot foothills, making its torturous way up
to the Antelope bench, where Jud Benson ran his
small ranch.

Wes pulled out of the brakes a little after noon
and started the climb through the canyons. Here
the trail was barely wide enough for a buckboard.
On either side were steep, boulder-strewn slopes.
It was a savage country, Wes was thinking, suited
to a man of Benson's flinty disposition.

Rounding a hairpin turn in the trail, Wes suddenly pulled up. There, ahead of him, was a huge
boulder covering the entire width of the road.

For a moment, Wes looked at it, and while he
was still watching, he heard a rumble far down the
trail behind him. He reined his pony around and
turned back until he could see his back-trail. Several hundred yards below him, another big boulder
had been rolled onto the trail.

For a second, he just stared at it, and then he knew
he was trapped. Even as he thought it, he heard
the earth-shaking boom of dynamite. Swiveling his
head toward the top of the slope, he looked just in

time to see the whole top of the rimrock lifted off slowly into the sky.

It landed on the slope above him in a long, muffled thunder, and then the landslide began. Through Wes's mind flashed only one thought, "So Barney Lothar *is* behind it."

He slipped out of the saddle and looked around him. To escape over the cliff was impossible. To reach either boulder barrier and climb over was equally impossible. And the mounting, earth-pounding thunder was fast approaching— bringing death.

Wes looked up. Twenty yards ahead was a massive granite boulder. Without another thought, he scrambled to it and dived for its shelter, just as the vanguard of leaping, pounding rocks reached him. Crouching in the lee of the huge boulder he waited breathless, as all hell broke loose around him. In a mad fury of noise, the slide pounded past him, over him, on all sides of him, battering the earth in giant kiting leaps. A stifling fog of dust smothered him as buckets of dirt sifted down. Great boulders leaped over the top of the one he was crouching under, and he saw them land in a smear of sparks, leaving a stink of brimstone behind them. Once, he felt his protective boulder move, and he thought he was lost, but it settled back again into its deep pocket.

The long keening shrill of his horse rose over the thunder and then died, and Wes felt a little sick. Suddenly, the thunder muted and then was gone, but Wes did not move. He realized that whoever had set the dynamite off would be down to look at the job he had done.

Several inches of dust covered him, and Wes

knew that the camouflage would be to his advantage, so he remained utterly still.

Presently, far down the slope, he saw a band of horsemen on the trail. They pulled up to the spot where the road had been, and looked down into the canyon. Apparently satisfied, they reined away and rode off, but not before Wes recognized the leader as Jud Benson.

Slowly, Wes unearthed himself from the inches of dust and gravel and looked around and below him. The road was no more. The slope made one unbroken line from the top to the canyon floor. Somewhere, under thousands of tons of rock and dirt down there, his horse was buried—and so was he, Barney Lothar would think.

Wes worked his way to the top of the slope and sat down, rolling a smoke, thinking. No one except Barney Lothar knew he was coming to Benson's today, so this had been planned by Barney and Benson—a neat piece of dry-gulching with no evidence of foul play, only the indication that Wes had been on a narrow mountain road when a landslide occurred.

"Then I'll stay dead," Wes thought, grinning a little. "Here's one ghost that's goin' to do plenty of hauntin'."

He worked his way down to Lost River, swam it after dark. Next morning, he spotted a band of horses on the edge of the brakes. By maneuvering for an hour, he drove five of them into a box canyon, the open end of which he filled with brush. It took him the rest of the day to catch a crippled old mare, branded Chain Link. Once he had her, he fashioned a hackmore out of his belt. That night he made his slow way to Doubletree under the welcome cover of darkness.

Lucy lived in the rooms over her restaurant, and it was here that Wes made for. He let himself in the door at the top of the back stairway and surprised Lucy reading.

"Oh, it's you, Wes. Why all the tiptoeing?" she asked, rising and coming over to him.

Wes told her, and learned that the news of his death had not yet reached town. Lucy received the news of Barney's guilt with a knowing look; and then she said, "Well, my fine deputy, what's the next move for the Ghost of Doubletree?"

"Plenty," Wes said grimly. "I'm hidin' out in a cave in Echo Canyon, over south. You've got to get me a saddle, a good horse and ammunition. Also, you've got to see me every day and tell me what Lothar is planning to do, who he picks for his deputies, what he aims to do about Reardon. I got a hunch this is goin' to break—and when it does, this ghost is goin' to buy into the game."

Nightly, Lucy brought her messages. From her three trips, Wes had learned this much: that Benson reported the landslide and that Barney sent out a search party for Wes; that Barney had appointed two deputies, a couple of honest, respected men who wanted to clean up the country; that Reardon was still in jail, and that Moley was as determined as ever to saddle him with the crime of trying to kill Wes.

The fourth night, Lucy rode up to the cave, and Wes met her in the dark, his face unshaven, his clothes smelling of smoke and tobacco.

"It's come at last, I think," Lucy told him, as she sat beside him on a rock. "Barney Lothar claims to be convinced that this gang of rustlers is working in the south end of the county now. Several reports of missing beef, night riders, and shootings have come in to Barney's office. He's organizing a big posse on the quiet, and taking them down to hunt over those badlands next to the border.''

"When?"

"Starting tomorrow, so Loosh Moley told me when he was in to supper tonight.''

Wes said nothing for a moment; he was thinking. "So all the best men in the county are headin' south with Barney." He looked at her. "What does that mean to you?"

"That all rustling hell's going to break loose in the north end of the county,'' she said, just as a man would have said it.

Wes grinned and patted her hand. "Smart girl. There'll be a bunch of raids and quick drives, and me, I've got a hunch this time those rustled beef aren't goin' to be driven through the brakes and a hundred miles north and two counties away.''

"Why?"

"Because every last man that can fight is goin' along with Barney. There won't be anyone left here, so why sneak when you can walk?''

"I don't get it," Lucy said.

"Just this. In the next county, there's a town of Antelope Mound. Ever hear of it?"

"Stupid," Lucy said, laughing at his teasing. "It's the county seat.''

"Sure. It's got a railroad. Remember?"

"The same one we have. What of it?"

Wes said nothing for a moment. Then he rose. "Reckon you could get hold of Barney Lothar's posse and have 'em back on the day I wire you to have 'em?"

Lucy said, after a moment's thought, "Yes. Why? Where will you wire from?"

Wes only laughed and put out his hand to help her up. "A man has got to have some secrets. You go on back now."

As soon as Lucy was gone, Wes went over to his horse, which was staked out in the thick piñon atop the mesa. He saddled up and rode off west. That was on Monday night.

Tuesday, before dawn, the posse assembled at an outlying ranch and headed south, riding all day and far into the night, on trails that were seldom traveled.

Tuesday night, Wes was hunkered down by a line-camp shack belonging to the Rocking K. Below him, in the grassy basin of a park visible in the moonlight, was a sleek herd of whitefaces— unherded, because all the Rocking K hands were riding with Acting-Sheriff Lothar. Wes sat there for a couple of hours, watching the cattle feed and bed down. Close to midnight, they started to stir and soon they were all on their feet. Then Wes heard the sharp cries of riders, who started to bunch and drive them.

That was all he wanted to know. He got his horse, and rode west all that night and the next day. Close to evening, he arrived at Antelope Mound, a tiny county-seat town squatting in dust and alkali and sagebrush on the rim of the desert. It's single street of weathered stores held little activity.

Wes rode straight to the station and sent a wire to Lucy at Doubletree. It read: "Have him back by Friday noon."

When Lucy received the telegram, she hurried over to the station and sent a wire to Mica City, a tiny waystation at the southern tip of the county. Moley had told her before he left that Mica City would be the spot from which the posse would work. Her telegram read: "Reardon has confessed. Imperative posse return as brakes hideout is disclosed." Lucy signed the name, Max Lothar.

"But you ain't Max Lothar, Miss Lucy," the telegrapher said.

Lucy smiled a little. "Jake, you used to own a couple of hundred head of cattle on shares, didn't you?"

"Sure."

"How many have you now?"

The telegrapher said, wryly, "Ten."

"You want to know who took them?"

Jake's eyes widened, and his voice deepened. "I'd like to lay my hands on the gent."

"Then send that wire," Lucy said. "If an answer comes to Max Lothar, let me see it first."

Wes hung around the Glory Hole saloon in Antelope Mound until Thursday night. Thursday afternoon, a full train of empty cattle cars puffed into Antelope Mound and pulled up by the stockpens. By evening, the first herd of beef was hazed through the town. They wore the Chain Link brand, but their drivers were not Chain Link hands.

Wes, who regarded them from inside the batwing doors of the Glory Hole, returned to the bar. In one day, he had become friends with the sleepy bartender.

"I'm ridin'," he said. "Reckon you'd do me a favor?"

"What is it?"

"I lost a bet with the boys that are loadin' this train out here tonight—two cases of whiskey. Reckon when the train is loaded, you'd deliver a couple of cases of whiskey to the caboose?"

."Hell, yes," the bartender said, and asked shrewdly, "They expectin' it?"

Wes grinned. "If they don't get it, they'll come in and tear your place down. Gimme a pencil and a piece of paper."

The bartender complied, and Wes wrote, "To the boys, from the Chief."

Then he paid for the whiskey, went out and got his horse. He made his way south, following the tracks and the rim of the desert. There was a small divide the train had to cross, he remembered, before it dropped down to the basin and joined the line from Doubletree.

He arrived at the divide, a deep cut in a high rocky ridge, about midnight, and dismounted. He yanked the saddle off his horse and turned him loose. Then, in a small rincón over the ridge, he built a fire and squatted before it, musing.

A good two hours passed before he heard the laboring pant of the train making its way up the grade. He smothered his fire and walked over toward the cut. Presently, he saw the glare of the headlamp, which approached with the speed of a snail.

"A heavy pull," Wes thought, and grinned a little.

In a few minutes, the train pulled abreast of him, laboring mightily to make the top of the grade, which was only a hundred yards off. Wes waited until the locomotive and tender were past him, then he slid down the bank, ran a ways on the track-bed shoulder, grabbed the rungs of a loaded cattle car and pulled himself to the top. Carefully, he made his way up to the first cattle car, then jumped over to the tender and sat down on its cold iron.

The train clattered down the grade on this side of the ridge, picking up speed. Fifteen minutes later, it was on the flats and almost to the junction where it would join the line from Doubletree.

Wes rose, took a look down the top of the cars and saw no one. With a prayer that the two cases of whiskey were doing duty with the boys who had been picked to take the beef in, Wes drew his guns and climbed up over the coal. Below him, he could see the engineer and fireman, each in his seat at the cab windows. He slowly skidded down the coal until he was standing on the steel apron between the tender and the cab. Neither the engineer nor the fireman had seen him yet.

He said, "Howdy, gents."

They both turned, and the first thing they looked into were the yawning barrels of Wes's two guns.

It was the engineer who spoke first. He said drily, "No baggage car on tonight, fella, only cattle. You're out of luck."

"They'll do," Wes drawled, and added, "How soon you come to the Y and join the line that goes to Doubletree?"

"We ain't goin' to Doubletree," the engineer said. "We're goin' west."

"You're goin' east—to Doubletree," Wes said gently. "How far to the Y?"

The engineer looked at the fireman, speechless. Wes nosed up his gun and cocked it.

"Three-four minutes," the fireman said.

"You got a brakie on this train?" Wes asked.

"Sure."

"All right. When you get to the Y, I want you to get off this spur, stop the train, and start backin' her into Doubletree before that brakie can get up here. You savvy that?''

"What for?" the engineer argued reasonably. "You can't steal a trainload of cattle, son."

"Never mind that. You do what I say!"

The fireman started to grin. "The Doubletree spur ain't clear."

"You lie, fella," Wes said calmly, and cocked the other gun and pointed it at the fireman. "Do I have to shoot you to show you I mean business, you knothead? That spur is clear till noon tomorrow."

The fireman gulped. They had started to round a curve, and the engineer said pleadingly, "Listen. I've got to stop here at the Y. The brakie throws the switch shut, or we don't go to Doubletree."

"Does he always?"

"Sure. He closes it."

"Good. I just don't want him up here. When he gets it throwed shut, you start backin' up—and don't stop!'

They were slowing down now. The engine went on another fifty yards, then stopped, and the engineer peered out and back. Wes kept his eyes on the two.

When the engineer got the highball from the brakie, he turned despairingly to Wes. "I'm tellin' you, son, he'll be back here in ten minutes."

"Let him come," Wes said gently. "Fog it."

After a laboring start, the train started to back up, slowly, gathering speed.

Wes waited until it was well under way, then moved down on the steps, up into the cab, where he could still cover the crew and be out of the line of vision of the brakie.

He didn't have long to wait. A shout came from

the top of the tender, and soon the brakie was skidding down the coal, swearing hoarsely. "You gone loco, Bailey! Hell, do you know where you're goin'?" he shouted.

And suddenly, by his side, appeared Jud Benson, a pinched man in tattered, greasy range clothes, his face set in a vicious snarl. His hand was poised over the butt of his gun.

"Stop this train!" he barked.

"Easy," Wes said gently, and both Benson and the brakie wheeled to confront him. As Benson recognized him, he took a step backwards, his face draining to a dirty white.

Wes said, "Yeah, it's me, Benson. Not a ghost. I don't kill easy."

Benson licked his lips and Wes stepped closer to him. "You stink, Jud," he drawled. "Clear out of here. I don't like to look at you."

When Benson started up the coal, Wes said, "Not that way. Just go down the steps."

"But—but the train's goin'," Benson said. "I'll break a leg."

"I hope so," Wes said calmly, although he knew he wouldn't, for the train was not traveling fast and the right of way was as flat as a table. "I almost broke my leg once, too. Remember? That was when a mountain happened to fall on me."

Benson turned and looked out at the night. Then, slowly, he walked down the steps. Wes saw him jump, and then he turned to the crew. "Sit up on the seats, boys. This'll last all night."

It did—and through the next morning too. The brakie slept, after informing Wes the punchers were all dead drunk, and Wes, on the seat back of the engineer, had a hard time to keep from drowsing.

At sun-up, the four of them shared breakfast, for the engineer had long since resigned himself.

Close to noon, Wes saw they were on the long slope down into Doubletree. He said, "Tie down that whistle, fella. I aim to announce myself."

The engineer did as he was bid. The screeching train rattled backwards at a smart clip down the slope. Wes said, "Pull up at the station." And then he ran up the coal to the tender, where he could see.

The whistle was getting results. People started running for the station, and a good many of them were men. Strangely, the whole county seemed to be in Doubletree today, and Wes guessed it was because of the twin news of the posse's return and the new rustling.

Slowly, the train backed into the station, and Wes jumped down. With both guns out, he ran for the caboose, which was just flush with the station platform. He arrived just as the first puncher, eyes bleared with drink, poked his head off the back platform, his mouth agape.

Wes took the puncher's guns, booted him down into the babbling crowd, and then went inside the caboose. The other hands were all sleeping. He woke them by shooting through the roof. They came out of the bunks with a yell, and in another minute they were lined up on the platform, hands over head.

Wes looked at the crowd, which now was in a seething uproar. In it, he saw Moley, fighting his way to the front, alongside Barney Lothar. A dozen dusty possemen followed.

Moley took one look at Wes and cursed in amazement. "McGrew!" He gestured to the train and said, "What's this, McGrew?"

Instead of answering, Wes holstered his guns and waited until Barney Lothar was standing beside Moley. "This?" Wes echoed gently. "Why, ain't you ranchers missed some cattle in the last couple of days?"

"Certainly," Moley said slowly. "What's that got to do with this?"

Wes jerked a thumb to the train of bawling cattle. "There they are. Take a look at the brands."

A dozen men broke into the cars and verified Wes's story. Then Wes turned to Barney Lothar, whose face seemed carved in white granite.

"Ain't you got somethin' to say, Barney?" he asked gently.

Barney grinned weakly. "Yes. I'm glad you're alive, Wes, and this was mighty pretty work."

"Nothin' else to say?" Wes prompted.

"Sure. Let's unload and look at 'em".

"Not yet, Barney," Wes rapped out, as Barney started to duck through the crowd. "Come over here."

Lothar could not escape. He was hemmed in by people, but he kept up the bluster to the last.

"This gent Barney, our sheriff," Wes said dryly, "is the cattle thief, Moley. These are all his boys, his gunmen. He tolled all you jaspers down south there so they could raid your spreads, drive off your herds to Antelope Mound and ship 'em out before you got back. Ask him about it."

"Careful, whelp!" Barney growled. His hand dropped to his gun butt. "That's a damn lie! You can never prove it!" He turned to the men. "You ever seen me before, you men?"

Their denial was genuine, anyone could see.

"What was the name of your leader, boys?" Wes asked. "Benson, wasn't it? Jud Benson?"

They nodded surlily.

"And Benson," Wes continued, "talked before he died, Barney. He talked plenty—enough to put a rope around your neck anyway."

"Bluff," Barney sneered.

Slowly, Wes turned to the engineer, who had been listening to all this. "Railroader," Wes said mildly, "what did Mr. Benson say before he jumped the train? Did he say that Barney Lothar was behind this?"

The engineer looked at him gravely, a twinkle in his eye. "He did," he lied calmly. "Benson said Lothar was his boss."

"Didn't he say that Lothar brought his gunies over from the brakes to try and gulch me and thereby throw the blame on Reardon, who'd be put in jail, giving Barney a free hand to organize this posse and leave the county to his rustlers?"

"He did," the engineer said. "He said that and lots more."

"Yeah. For instance, that all this rustlin' that's been goin' on here for a year couldn't be stopped because Barney Lothar knew every move the law was goin' to make. Is that right?"

"That's right," the engineer lied again.

Wes turned, his mouth open, to address Lothar, but the warning in Barney's eyes was enough. It was a signal, never spoken, but understood.

Barney streaked for his guns, at the same time leaping for the shelter of the caboose platform. He shot first, wildly, on the run. Wes, both guns out now, raised one, and emptied it in a chattering blast, just as Barney reached the rear platform.

Then Barney disappeared, but Wes did not move.

He smiled a little, his guns at his sides. "Go see," he said to Moley.

Moley climbed the platform. Lothar had been thrown clear across the platform by the blast of lead. He lay on his face in the cinders on the other side of the train his blood slowly soaking into the dirt.

Moley turned to the crowd. "He's dead—and good riddance!"

In all the wild excitement that followed, Wes only knew one thing, that Lucy's arms were around his neck, and that a thousand men were pounding his back sore.

When it had quieted down some, Moley said, with heartfelt sincerity, "Wes, by seniority, you're the sheriff of this county. And so help me, if we ever vote you out of office, it'll be to vote you into the governorship of the Territory!"

Wes looked down at Lucy. "Reckon you'd like to be a sheriff's wife?"

Lucy said, "Reckon I will if I'm asked," and she was in his arms.

Over Lucy's shoulder, Wes saw the engineer grinning. He winked at him, and the engineer winked back.

"I wisht I could wait here a day," the engineer said drily, chuckling. "I'd name this dang train of mine the Honeymoon Special."

Death Cold-Decks
a Tinhorn

The five men pulled up their horses at a bend in the sandy road. "There's the county line, you hombres," the sheriff said. "Let's see how fast you can cross it."

He was talking to Tom Band, big in a frock coat, who up to now had possessed all the brassy assurance of a medicine show barker, and to Tip Hale, Tom's companion. It was young Tip Hale who flushed to the very roots of his chestnut hair, for this was the prime indignity in the cattleland. These men did not think them even worth shooting.

Tom Band took a deep breath and said pompously, "Sirs, you will regret this. You will live to see the day when—"

"Come on, Tom," Tip said, warned by the sheriff's look.

"You will live to see the day—" Tom started again.

The sheriff raised the shotgun held across his lap and growled, "If you don't git the hell out of here, you won't live to see any day I live to see. Now drag it!"

Tom wheeled his horse around with all the dignity he could muster, and he and Tip trotted off. But when they had ridden only a few yards, Tom, wise to the ways of the law, looked over his shoulder. Then he dug his spurs in his bay, hunkered down over his horse's neck and yelled, "Ride Tip!"

The blast of a shotgun came on the heel of his warning. Tom raised up in his saddle, howled mightily—and kept on riding. Two minutes later, when they had achieved the far bend in the road and were screened by a jutting heap of malpais, they pulled up and dismounted. Gingerly, Tom pulled off his frock coat. Underneath it he was wearing only the starched front of a shirt over his tattered underwear. He slowly took off tie, collar and shirtfront, then peeled off the upper half of his underwear and turned his broad and bleeding back to Tip.

"How's it look?" he asked.

"Like you'd got shot," Tip growled.

He was seated on a rock, glaring morosely at Tom. Under twenty-five, lean, his face burned an oak brown by the desert suns, Tip Hale had the look of and wore the dress of a thirty-a-month cowpuncher. He would fool anybody who didn't take the trouble to look at his hands. They gave him away. They were uncalloused, slim-fingered, the hands of a man who does no physical toil. They were rolling a cigarette now.

"Them polecats!" Tom growled.

He swore sulphurously. His broad, crafty face wore an unconvincing scowl. Tom Band was not only a man who didn't hold grudges, but he was a sensible man. He knew he deserved what he had just received. And, with the easy philosophy of the professional sharper, he dismissed it. His round, florid face held a look of shrewdness as he glanced at Tip now, and replaced the threadbare coat on his smarting back.

"Well, I reckon we worked out that bunch," he observed cheerfully.

"That's three times in a month," Tip said quietly.

Tom shrugged. "They're a hard-headed lot down this way."

"Too hard-headed for a shell game," Tip said quietly. "Who ain't?"

Tom glanced up, a hurt look on his face. "Why, we done all right so far," he said.

"How much money you got?" Tip countered.

"Why—er—none."

"Neither have I. Does that sound all right to you?"

Tom turned to confront Tip. "What's the matter, kid? Ain't you satisfied?"

"No," Tip answered quietly. "Ever since I can remember, I been a come-on for your games, Tom. I been run out of so many towns I've lost track. I've spent most of my life hungry and sleepin' in hay stacks. I ain't been honest for so long I wouldn't know how it felt."

"Honest?" Tom echoed. "You mean you'd like to be one of these tank-town hicks that gets trimmed every time he leaves nursin' cattle on a Saturday night?"

"Who just got trimmed?" Tip asked drily. He rose and looked around him and threw away his cigarette. "Well, Tom, I think I'll drag it. You and me have just about wore out our partnership. You can stick to this gyp game. Me, I aim to do some honest work, just to see how it feels."

Tom glanced at him shrewdly and then sighed. "All right," he said quietly. "Hell, I might of known it! I get you broke in just right, get you all set for a big killin', and then you walk out on me—me and about eight thousand dollars."

Tip said jeeringly, "Eight thousand dollars! Tom, you'll never see that much money."

"Not now," Tom agreed sadly.

"You never will."

"Maybe not," Tom said mournfully. "I made a mistake. If I'd of had a partner with any guts, I would of, though."

Tip flushed. These were the old tactics Tom used, and ones that always succeeded in making Tip so mad that he gave in. He could see it coming, knew that this was just the preface to a new scheme of Tom's. But it made him mad, just the same.

"I got as much guts as you have, you big slob!" Tip said angrily. "I reckon if there's any fightin' to be done, I always do it."

Tom waved a negligent hand. "Not that kind of guts," he said idly. "I meant gamblin' guts. You just ain't got 'em."

"Have you?"

"I reckon. If I had a man to help me, I could swing the biggest deal of my life right now."

"If there's money in it," Tip snapped, "I'm in on it! I've got kicked around so long I'm just about due for a piece of loot."

Tom said slyly, "Then you were just shootin' off your mouth a minute ago?"

"I reckon," Tip murmured. "Now what's the scheme?"

"You'll stick with me through this?"

Tip nodded. "But only this time. If I have any

money when I'm through, I'm pullin' out, Tom. That's a promise."

"Shake on it. That's a promise."

They shook hands solemnly in the middle of the road, and then suddenly Tom grinned. His old bravado was back. He reached in a hip pocket and, with a flourish, drew out a newspaper.

"This," he announced solemnly, "is our fortune, younker. It's the Tascosa Enterprise."

"A newspaper!" Tip sneered. "Where'd you get it?"

"Back there in Pinto Wells. But did you ever hear of Puerco?"

"No."

"It's on the other side of the Capitans," Tom said mysteriously, gesturing to the line of blue mountains to the west. "It's a stage junction. The north-south and east-west stages stop there."

"What of it?"

"They tell me there's a poker game been goin' on in the single saloon there for five years."

"Five years!" Tip echoed. "Hell, it can't be."

"It has," Tom said. "Folks get off the north-bound stage to go west, and they got to wait over a day. So they sit in the poker game. Folks come and folks go, and they usually leave money. The game's been goin' on for five years."

"Well, what of it?" Tip asked impatiently.

For answer, Tom reached down and pulled off a boot. He stuck a hand in it and fished around for several seconds, then drew forth a wad of banknotes. When Tip saw them, he swore angrily, but Tom held up his hand.

"Easy, son! Sure, I been holdin' out on you. But we needed capital to swing this deal." He extended the banknotes. "There's two hundred dollars. A hundred of it's yours. You take a stage to Puerco and git in that poker game. And boy, you got to win money. You got to win another couple hundred dollars. Think you can do it?"

"If I'm lucky," Tip said.

"Good! That'll give us the capital to work on. And now take a look at this." He spread the paper out on the road, and the two of them talked. They talked for an hour. Finally, when they rose, Tip was grinning.

"What do you think?" Tom said.

"I think it's a keno," Tip murmured. "Man, if it'll only work! We'll be rich!"

"Unh-hunh," Tom nodded, his shrewd eyes greedy. "We will."

Tip hadn't been in Puerco an hour before he saw that Tom was right about the poker game. It never stopped. Puerco itself was a string of weather-beaten buildings flanking a desert road. Only the Exchange House and the Indian Head showed any signs of prosperity, for they fattened on the forced idleness of travelers. The poker game itself was going on at a round, green-felted table in the back of the Indian Head saloon. It was the only gambling game in the place, and it was played by a gang of local experts.

One of these was Jody Hartnett, the county sheriff, who had worn out three chairs and increased his waist measurement from thirty-six to forty-four in countless thousands of hours of poker. He was a quiet man, with a big head and the most heartless eyes Tip had ever seen. His poker was machine-like, flawless, but Tip had the uncomfortable feeling that he would kill a man with as little emotion as he would take a pot. The other two local players seemed awed by him.

They had played four hours of poker, with Tip feeling his way and keeping his mouth shut, when a newcomer walked up to the table. Jody Hartnett looked up, and over his heavy slack face came the suggestion of a smile.

He looked at the new man, a broad-shouldered, husky puncher about Tip's age. The puncher wore a defiant look, as if he was certain before he sat down that he would not be welcome in this game.

"Any room, Jody?" he asked sullenly.

"Well, well, another cub!" Hartnett drawled. "Goin' to show us who invented the game, son?"

"You know damn well I ain't," the newcomer growled.

"Sure, I do," Hartnett agreed. "Maybe these other jaspers don't, though." To Tip he said, "Meet the ranny that never won a pot in his life, Hale. This is Dolf Connors."

Connors shook hands limply and drew up a chair, and the game got under way again. Tip could feel the enmity between these two men, but he did not have the leisure to speculate on it, for immediately the game settled down to a cut-throat business.

At the end of the first day, Tip had won a hundred and fifty dollars. At three the following afternoon, he excused himself and strolled down the street. He'd won another hundred dollars today—two fifty in all. He decided that things were shaping up.

Remembering Tom's instructions, he drifted down-street, searching for the post office. He found it, a one-room cubby hole jammed between a saddle shop and the Puerco Emporium. Entering, he walked to the wicket and slapped loudly on the counter. He was in high spirits, with more money in his pockets than he had ever had before.

A girl was suddenly framed in the wicket. "Do you have to batter the place down?" she inquired coldly.

Tip stared, and then removed his hat. He couldn't remember ever having seen such lovely hair, such red lips, such blue, blue eyes, but he was used to the sharp speech she used. Indeed, he had come to expect sharpness in everyone's speech.

"All right, sister," he said placatingly. "Take it easy. I didn't see you."

"I'm not your sister," the girl said. "Keep a civil tongue in your head."

Tip grinned. "Reckon that goes both ways, then," he drawled.

For a moment they glared at each other, and then the girl laughed shortly. "All right. I guess I was a little sharp."

"What's the matter? No business?" Tip asked more pleasantly.

She looked strangely at him. "Why would that make me sharp?"

"I dunno. Why?"

"What is it you want?" she asked, her voice suddenly chill.

"A envelope and stamp."

She gave them to him. He pulled out a handful of gold and flipped a coin to her. She looked at the heap of shining coins he had in his hand, and then raised her glance to him. She frowned slightly.

Tip caught the expression of disapproval on her face. "What's the matter? Don't you like money here?"

"I don't like gambling money anywhere," the

girl said bluntly. "I suppose that's where you got it—at the poker game. At least, I've seen you around town for two days now."

The girl's blue eyes regarded him icily.

"That's right. What's wrong with my gamblin'?"

"Nothing," the girl said. "I—I hate to lose money at it."

"You gamble yourself, then?" Tip asked.

"Hardly. But part of that money you've got there is my brother's. He's gambling, too."

"Who's he?" Tip asked, and added cockily, "Maybe I can ease up on him."

"You'd hardly do that," said the girl. "Good day."

Out on the street again, Tip grinned.

So her brother was in the poker game! Then that must be Dolf Connors, the gent who was losing his pants. Tip shook his head and went into the Emporium. There, he got all his gold changed into banknotes, stuffed them in the envelope, addressed the letter to Charles Baden, care of General Delivery, Puerco, and went back to the game.

Two hours later, the stage came in. Within five minutes, Tip heard Tom Band's loud and hearty voice. Soon Tom strolled into the bar. A sudden transformation had taken place. Tom was dressed in an elegant black suit, and he carried a cane. A diamond stud—glad, of course—flashed in his shirt front. He was smoking a cigar a foot long, and he had the air of a prosperous traveler. His first act was to set up drinks for the house, his second to stroll over to the poker table.

After a moment's watching, he announced loudly, "Gentlemen, is there room for another chair here perhaps?"

"Always room for one more," Jody Hartnett drawled. "Pull one up."

Then Tom introduced himself. "Charlie Baden's the name, gents." He shook hands all around. When he came to Tip, he gave no sign that he had seen him before.

Then the game started. It was soon obvious to all the players that this stranger, Charlie Baden, was no poker player. He was rash, curious and stubborn; in other words, a perfect sucker. By supper, they had cleaned him of a hundred dollars. After supper, the game was resumed, and Baden continued to lose. Tip winced to see the money which he had left at the post office in Charlie Baden's name being slowly but irrevocably lost. At nine, Baden was broke. He said, "Look here, gents. I've got some jewelry on me. I'd like to cash it for money. Anybody interested?"

Jody Hartnett slowly shook his head. "I reckon not, mister. This is a cash game here."

Baden bit his lip. His honest, broad face was set stubbornly. "All right. I'm a part owner in a gold mine down south. How'd it be if I put that up?"

"What mine?" Hartnett drawled coldly.

"Glory Hole."

"Where's that?"

"Down Tascosa way."

Jody shook his head. "I reckon not, stranger. We've never saw the mine. Maybe it's no good."

Baden shrugged and stood up. "Well, that's that," he said morosely and left the table.

Hartnett said, "What kind of suckers does he take us for?"

"Wait a minute," Tip put in slowly. "What did he say his name was?"

"Baden, Charlie Baden, wasn't it?" Dolf Connors said.

Tip turned to Hartnett. "You got last week's Tascosa *Enterprise* around anywhere?"

"Maybe. Why?"

"Reckon you could get it? I just remembered readin' somethin'."

Hartnett called the bartender, who soon supplied the paper. Tip spread it out on the table and began to read it. Soon he put his finger on a story and said, "Look at this, I thought so."

"Read it," Hartnett said curiously.

Tip read: "Strictly authoritative information from the Capitan field has it that the Glory Hole has hit a real pay streak. Manager Jupe Hawley is in a strange predicament, he says. He has been unable to locate either of his owners, Charles Baden of Billings, Montana, and Abel Stubbs, of Miles City, Montana, to inform them of their good luck. Hawley said he received instructions last month to close down the mine if pay ore wasn't struck. It's struck, but where are the owners? Jupe wants to know."

Tip finished reading and looked up at Jody Hartnett. "Hell!" Tip said. "I bet that's where he's goin' now."

"Wait a minute," Jody drawled softly. "This only come out about four days ago. They couldn't get word to Billings to this Baden gent in that time."

"That's right, too," Tip said.

Jody leaned forward and looked at the four men around the table. Tip was the only stranger playing now. "Maybe we're on to somethin' now," Jody said quietly.

"Like what?" Dolf Connors asked.

"Why, it don't seem like this Baden knows his

mine struck a pay streak. If he did, he wouldn't offer to put it up for a poker bet. Let's call the jasper back, have him put a figure on his mine, and we'll buy it. Then we'll win it back from him and have a hell-roarin' good gold mine to split between us.''

Dolf Connors' face was the only one that reflected distaste. He said abruptly, "That's forked, Jody."

Jody turned cold eyes on him. "Forked, hell! He made the proposition. We never. If he can't take care of his own business, it ain't our duty to take care of it for him, is it? Besides," he added drily, "you ain't in shape to turn down money now, Dolf, are you?"

Connors flushed. "Not exactly."

"All right. You keep still. I'll see if I can swing this." To Tip he said, "Gimme that paper."

Jody rose and went over and shoved the paper in the corner stove, then moved his massive bulk into the lobby. Presently he returned with Tom, who walked up to the table and addressed the players, with a note of eagerness in his voice.

"Is this right, gents? You aim to take this mine deed?"

"That depends," Tip observed casually. "What's the thing worth?"

"Well, I put fifteen thousand in it. I reckon I'll let it go for eight."

"How do we know this in on the level?" Tip asked.

Tom flushed. "Sir," he said ominously, "no one in this world has ever doubted Charlie Baden's word."

"All right, all right," said Tip. "You goin'
down there now?"

"Yes."

"What for?"

"Well, frankly, to sell it," Tom blurted out.
"It's taking too much of my money and not giving
enough in return."

"Let's see the deed," Jody Hartnett said. "Hell,
we're all honest here. We'll take your word for it,
Baden."

Tom disappeared. So did Jody and the two other
players. In five minutes they were all back. Tom
showed a worn deed, signed and stamped and
authentic looking, in spite of the fact that it was
only a four-day-old forgery. The players pretended
to examine it, and then they put out their money.
There was eight thousand dollars there on the table,
and it made Tip shiver to see it all.

Tom picked it up and rammed it in his pocket.
"Gentlemen, I'll gamble again, then, until my
stage comes."

"That's midnight," Jody Hartnett said.

But Tom's poker suddenly improved. When the
stage rolled in, he had lost only a hundred dollars,
and that to Tip.

They called the game off then. Jody Hartnett
could scarcely keep the smile off his face as he
shook hands with Tom. Tip had announced a day
ago that he was waiting for the south-bound stage,
so it did not seem strange that the two of them got
on the stage together.

While Tom was upstairs, getting his warbag,
Jody Hartnett got a notary over and gave Tip a
deed to his share of the mine.

"And mind you," Jody's parting words were,
"don't talk to this jasper."

Tip grinned. "Hell, why would I? I'll keep my mouth shut."

"You'd better," Jody said meaningly, "At least, until he gets out of ridin' distance from here."

When the stage finally rolled south out of Puerco, Tom lay back in his seat and roared. They were the only two passengers, so they could talk freely. Then and there, they made a division of spoils— four thousand dollars apiece. It was more than either of them had seen before in his whole life. Tip stuck his in the toe of his boot and sat back to listen to Tom Band's droll bragging.

Suddenly the brakes of the stage slammed on. Tom heard a man's voice out in the night yell, "Pull up there, Pokey!"

The stage careened to a halt, and Tip stuck his head out through the window. He could see two horsemen up by the swing team. They were talking in low tones to the driver, who had dismounted.

Then they all came back, and the driver opened the door.

"Pile outa there a minute, you two hombres," the driver said. "A gent out here wants to look you over."

Tom had a chance to give Tip's knee a warning squeeze before they climbed out. The driver was lighting a lantern, and when it finally caught and steadied to a glow, he swung it toward them and held it high.

"My dear sir," Tom said pompously, "if this is a holdup, you are unfortunate. If it's—"

"Yes," came a woman's voice, "he's the one, Dolf—the thin one there."

Then Dolf Connors' sister walked into the light.

Her face was stiff, filled with an implacable hatred. Dolf walked over to stand beside her, facing Tip.

"So it was a skin game," Dolf murmured. "You win a little money and mail it to Charles Baden. He picks it up at the post office, comes into the Indian Head and then you start your razzle-dazzle. He owns a mine. You remember his name. Perfect! We buy the mine and you two tin-horns run off with the money!"

Without waiting to explain further, Dolf Connors lashed out at Tip. The blow caught him flush on the shelf of the chin and sent him over backwards. He had no sooner landed than Connors was on top of him, wrenching his gun out of its holster. Then Dolf let Tip rise.

"Tin-horn, I aim to give you the trimmin' of your life," Dolf said gently. "First, though, I want the three hundred dollars I sunk in that phoney mine."

"My dear sir!" Tom expostulated. "Are you out of your head? This young chap—"

"Shut up!" Dolf rapped out. Then he said to the girl, "Linda, take my gun and keep that tub of lard covered."

The girl did, and then Dolf returned his attention to Tip. "Fork over."

"Go to hell!" Tip snarled.

"Son," Tom put in soothingly, "just three hundred dollars to avoid all this trouble. Hand it over to him and let's be on our way."

But Tip wasn't going to let his money go this easily. Something in his warped brain kept telling him that he deserved this, that he had suffered all these years to get it.

"And you go to hell, too!" he snarled at Tom.

"It's in his boot," Tom told Dolf.

But Dolf was not listening. He rushed at Tip, and Tip hung a right on his jaw that almost crushed his hand. Still, it didn't stop Dolf. A smashing hook to Tip's midriff jacknifed him, and an upper-cut straightened him out again, and then a dozen savage blows to the face pummeled every thought out of his mind. Dimly, Tip sensed that he was taking a beating, a bad beating, and that his slim, lean strength was no match for that of a man born and bred on a hard range country. He fought blindly, but it seemed as if he could never dodge the two-by-four that kept jabbing at his face. Mercifully, a blow behind the ear put him down. Then black-ness flooded into his mind and drowned it.

When he wakened, it was still dark. He was alone. The stage was gone; Tom was gone; the riders were gone. His right boot was off, and painfully he hauled himself to a sitting position and reached for it. Frantically, he reached inside for his money and found only a thin sheet of paper where the wad of banknotes had been.

With a trembling hand, he drew out the paper and turned it over. He could see writing on it, but he couldn't read it. It took him a full minute to fumble a match out of his pocket, and then he struck it and read the note:

I've taken three hundred dollars all told—one-fifty from you, one-fifty from your partner.
Dolf Connors

Below this, scrawled in a different hand, was added:

And I've taken the rest, you jug-headed sucker.
Tom Band

Tip never knew afterwards how he got through that day.

Without a horse, with every bone and muscle in his body aching, without food or water, he started to walk. He was afraid to follow the road lest he meet Dolf Connors' friends of the poker game. In his desperation, he followed the trail of the two horses, which cut off across the sage-stippled sand.

Tip did a lot of thinking that day. He couldn't get the contemptuous speech of Dolf Connors out of his head. All his cheap and tawdry life rolled out in review before him. He'd never made an honest penny, never made a friend; even Tom Band, almost lovable rascal that he was, had knifed him in the back at the last.

All that day, Tip thought of these things. But along toward evening, he couldn't think of them any longer. Food and water were the only things he could think about then.

He was approaching the foothills of the Capitans. He came across what looked like a ranch road, and he dragged along it till dark. He had to rest every half mile or so now, and his feet were blistered, his legs weary, and his tongue was out of his mouth.

It could have been midnight when he saw the lights. He didn't know. He did remember starting to yell, stumbling toward those lights. And suddenly they went out, and he felt his face in the dust. After that, he couldn't remember anything.

When he came to, there were two figures standing above him, and he was in a house. Slowly, as his eyes focused, he decided one of the figures was a girl. And then he decided it was Linda Connors, and he closed his eyes again, sure that he was in delirium. But when he looked up the sec-

ond time, there she was, clear this time, and her
face was only a little softer than when he had seen
it last.

"Well, you'll make it, all right," she said shortly.

"Where—where am I?" Tip asked.

"At our place—the Rocking L. Lord knows
how you got here! Didn't they take you on the
stage?"

Tip shook his head weakly. "They left—with
my money, too."

Linda almost smiled, then said curtly, "Good!
It serves you right."

All that day and the next, Linda brought him
food and drink, and he slept. Twice a day, morning and night, he saw Dolf Connors, who never
spoke to him. There was trouble in this house, Tip
could see. Dolf seldom spoke to Linda, and she, in
turn, seemed to be brooding about something.
Oftentimes, if Dolf did not come home till late,
Tip would hear her crying softly in the next room.

The third night, Tip heard her sobbing, and he
could stand it no more. He got out of bed, climbed
into his clothes and walked unsteadily but softly
into the next room. Linda sat at the kitchen table,
her head in her arms, crying as if her heart would
break.

For a moment, Tip didn't know what to do. He
cleared his throat. Linda whirled around in her
chair, and when she saw him, anger flushed into
her face.

"Oh, so you're a sneak, too?" she rapped out.

"I—I heard you cryin' in there," Tip said gently.
"I—shucks, I wondered if I could help."

"You might steal some money for us," Linda
said forlornly. When she saw the color mount in

Tip's face, she added, more gently, "I'm sorry. That wasn't very kind." She smiled a little sadly.

Tip said, "That's all right. You got no right to think well of me." He paused. "I'll clear out of here tonight, Miss Linda. It don't help things that you got to keep a sick man. Besides, I ain't sick. I guess I'll drag it."

"But you can't!" Linda cried. "You aren't well."

Tip was about to protest when his knees buckled under him. Linda helped him over to a chair, and he sat down, watching her as she sank into the chair opposite. Neither of them spoke for a moment. And Linda's face slowly settled into weariness.

"I heard you cryin' the other night too, Miss Linda," Tip said gravely. "Is there—what's wrong?"

She regarded his scarred, pale face. Beneath the brashness, the cockiness, the mocking, jeering insolence of a man who has always lived by his wits, there was something else—sympathy.

Linda shrugged. "You wouldn't understand."

"Try me."

Linda looked steadily at him. "Maybe you would, at that. I dare say you've wanted money badly."

"All my life."

Linda sighed. "Well, so do we. Oh, not money to spend. It's money to rescue—to rescue dad— that we need."

Tip siad nothing, waiting for her to go on.

"You see, a long time ago, when dad first took over the post office, he borrowed some money, government money, to gamble with. He lost it. He went to Mr. Hartnett—he's the sheriff, you know."

"Yeah, I know," Tip said coldly.

"It was a mistake. Mr. Hartnett paid the

shortage, but ever since he's held it over dad's head. Slowly but surely, he's ruined our ranch. He waited until dad made a little money and got the place, then he started borrowing from dad. Of course, he never paid any of it back. And always, there was that threat to expose dad. Finally, dad had to leave. He knew Hartnett would give him away. And now Hartnett owns the whole place, through mortages, and sooner or later he'll foreclose.''

''Where's your dad now?''

''Hiding out in the hills. He has been for a year.''

''Can't he come in?''

''No. We've said he's on a trip to Oregon. If he comes back, Hartnett will borrow more and more money, and when he has everything of ours, then he'll notify government agents—and dad will go to jail.''

Tip was quiet a moment. He knew what this meant to Linda. For himself, a jam like this would have meant nothing except a change of scenery, but he sensed that these Connors were proud people, proud of their name and their reputation for honesty.

''That's tough,'' he said finally. ''Is that why Dolf sat in the poker game that night?''

Linda nodded. ''We needed money desperately— to meet a note.''

''And you didn't get it.''

''No.''

For a long moment they were silent, and then Linda sighed. ''Well, we've got to take our medicine. Only it's—it's pretty bitter.''

Tip only nodded, and when Linda ordered him back to bed, Tip went docilely. He did a lot of thinking that night, and it was dawn before he slept.

He got up the next day. He worked around the place, splitting wood, hauling water. And all the time, his face was sober and reflective, so that Linda was almost sorry she'd mentioned their affairs.

Two days later Tip rose from the breakfast table and said, "Well, I reckon I'll hit the grit today." He was ill-at-ease.

"Suit yourself," Dolf said shortly.

"I—I ain't got no money," Tip stammered. "But when I get some, I'll pay you back."

Dolf rose and said, "Forget it," and walked out. Tip faced Linda alone.

"I—" Tip began, then bogged down. There was so much to say, and no way to say it. "If I was you," he said slowly, starting off on a new tack, "I wouldn't worry too much about this. It'll come out all right."

Linda impulsively put a hand on his arm and smiled a little. "It's nice of you to encourage us, Tip—but it's no use."

Tip flushed and shifted his feet. "Does that gang at the Indian Head know what me and Tom pulled?" he asked in a low voice. "Did Dolf tell 'em?"

"No. Why?"

"I just wondered if it'd be safe to hit town," Tip said evasively.

"I think so."

Tip nodded and put out a hand that had some work blisters on it. "Good bye—Linda."

Linda smiled "Good bye, Tip." She took his hand. "Tip, are you going back to your old ways?"

"I'm gettin' a job," Tip said grimly. "I'm through lookin' for easy money."

"Then bless you, Tip. You have a kind heart."

Tip ducked out. Dolf had a horse saddled for him at the corral, and he told Tip to leave it at the stable in town.

On the way to town, Tip took his time. It seemed to him that in these past few days, he'd been seeing things differently. For instance, why should he, a low-life saddle-tramp, a tin-horn, a man who never did an honest day's work in his life, get a better deal out of life that a jasper like Dolf? Here he was, free, broke, young, in good health, with not a care in the world—while back there were Dolf and Linda, chained to a life of hell and disgrace because of that crooked slob of a Jody Hartnett. It didn't tally up.

Riding into town, Tip was wary. He rode past the Indian Head and down the street, and gave his horse over to the feed stable attendant. He suddenly thought it was very funny that he didn't even have stage fare to clear out of Puerco, when any minute might bring back the news to Hartnett that the Glory Hole mine deed was a forgery. He thought it even funnier that he didn't give a damn. He only wanted money for one thing—a gun.

At the Puerco Emporium, he mixed with a crowd of punchers and prospectors loafing there. His nerves were slowly keying up to the old pitch. A bunch of punchers were gathered around the cold stove, and he took a seat on a cartridge box behind them. One man in particular Tip noticed, because he was a little drunk and because he wore twin Colts strapped to his hip.

There was a lot of horseplay among the punchers,

and under its cover Tip inched closer to the man with the two guns. He rolled smokes and waited, and then threw his cigarette away and drew out his tobacco sack again. It slipped from his fingers, down behind the packing case. Tip knelt down, to fumble for it. Once out of sight of the others, he reached up for the puncher's gun.

It had to be a quick and smooth job, and it was. Before he got up, the gun was tucked unobtrusively in his belt. Then he bought some tobacco and strolled out. Out on the board walk, he turned up toward the Indian Head, quickening his pace.

The thought of what he was about to do didn't excite him. It would be easy. Hell, many a man, when he was broke and down and out, stuck a gun to his head and pulled the trigger. Maybe it hurt, but anybody could stand pain. Then what was the difference between holding the gun yourself and having someone else hold it? One shot, and you were out. But he did wish he were a gun-fighter, a hair-trigger ranny who could make a gun talk. That would make it easier. But he knew he wasn't.

Tip shouldered through the swing doors of the Indian Head, and immediately saw that the poker game was in session. It was as if he had never left it. Jody Hartnett's gross, fat form overflowed the chair, and a cold, stinking cigar was clamped between his teeth.

Tip took a deep breath and strode over to the table. Hartnett didn't look up. Tip lifted a leg and kicked Hartnett's shin. The shock of it knocked the cigar out of Hartnett's mouth, and he jerked his head around to regard Tip.

"You big slob!" Tip said softly. "I went down to Tascosa. That jasper never owned that Glory

Hole mine. He was a phoney. And so are you. You and him was in cahoots to rim the rest of us.''

Hartnett slowly heaved his bulk out of the chair. "Who was in cahoots with who?''

"Don't talk, you big tub of guts!'' Tip grated. "Fill your hand!''

Before he was finished talking, he saw, with a kind of bleak despair, that Hartnett had been stalling until he was on his feet. His fat ham of a hand was already wrapped around his gunbutt. Tip clawed wildly at his own gun, but even before it cleared leather, he saw Hartnett's gun spout orange.

A savage hand seemed to grab Tip at the waist and whirl him around. Doggedly, he swung his own gun and fired. He fired blindly, desperately, feet planted apart. And when he felt the hammer click on the empty chamber, he raised the gun over his head and threw it at Hartnett. But the sheriff was not there to receive it. He was sprawled on his face, a mountain of flesh heaped on the sawdust of the barroom floor. Tip tried to grin with delight, but the next thing he knew, he was tasting the sawdust of the floor in his own mouth.

Men carried him into the Exchange House and upstairs. A doctor came in and fussed over him, hurting him like hell. They lighted lamps and then blew them out, and they gave him food. Then they left him alone. Nothing was distinct. He'd go to sleep with the patch of window showing blue sunlight. He'd wake a few minutes later, to find it showing black.

Then one morning he opened his eyes and saw Dolf and Linda Connors standing over him. At first, he tried to remember where this had happened before, but he couldn't. Then, just as before,

Dolf left and Linda came up to him. She knelt now. Close to her, Tip could see the tears in her eyes.

"Tip, you did it for us!" Linda said softly.

Tip nodded weakly. "It wasn't much. Hell, it's the only right thing I ever done in my life." He reached for her hand. "I'm glad I could do it before I die."

"But you won't die, Tip!" she said eagerly.

"No?"

"No. Oh, there's so much to tell you! After you killed Hartnett, the coroner went through his rooms. He's a wanted man, Tip. He killed three men fifteen years ago up in Idaho. He was a fugitive! And there's a five thousand reward out for him, Tip. It's yours."

Tip grinned weakly. "This ain't the way I figured it out, Linda. I thought he'd get me."

"But didn't you care, Tip?"

Tip looked into her blue yes. "No. I wasn't worth a damn. I—there was only one thing I wanted, Linda, and I couldn't have it."

"Peace of mind?"

"No. I had that already. I reckon." He paused and looked her straight in the eye. "It was you."

Linda smiled softly. "Have you ever asked me, Tip?"

Tip's mouth sagged open. "But I'm a tin-horn, honey."

Linda shook her head. "You're a right hombre, Tip—enough of a one that I love you, anyway."

It hurt Tip to kiss her, because he sat up to do it, But he didn't notice the pain.

War Fires Light the Stage Trails

It was late afternoon on the sixth day out of El Paso when the stage lurched to a halt.

The girl on the seat opposite Jim Cade sat utterly still a moment, her eyes closed, and then she roused herself. Her first act, Jim noticed covertly, was to brush the dust from her basque. That was an impossible chore because the white particles clung to the material. She looked around her.

After awhile she must have noticed the heat had let up for she smelled deeply of the mountain air. Somewhere up in the hills it had rained and the moist air seemed to bring color into her smooth cheeks.

She said pleasantly to Jim, "What is it now?"

The whiskey drummer next to Jim answered promptly, sourly, "It's just this stage line, miss. It don't need an excuse to stop."

The girl—Judith Elliot was her name—looked at Jim, and a light of amusement crept into her level blue eyes. She said nothing. Instead, she leaned out and looked up toward the horses. The stage had stopped on a gentle downslope. Beyond the lead team was an arroyo whose banks were filled with water racing away into the beginning dusk.

The driver, a burly man who had been with them since the station stop this morning, walked thoughtfully back up the slope and stopped at the window.

"Better light, folks," he said gruffly. "We'll be here the night."

He opened the door and Judy Elliot stepped unsteadily to the ground. Jim Cade followed her. Erect, he was a little over six feet tall, with wide shoulders fitted snugly into a broadcloth coat and an easy grace of movement that was deceptively indolent. He was smoking a thin cigar, which he removed from his mouth as he strolled down to the wash.

Four hours ago it had been a wide and sandy arroyo. Now it was running full, and some experience with these things told Jim Cade that it would continue to do so half the night.

He was not aware that Judy Elliot was close to him until she spoke.

"It doesn't seem bad, does it?"

"Not so bad," Jim agreed.

"Then why doesn't the driver go on?"

Jim smiled. "He's got a woman for a passenger, ma'am. I reckon it's against company rules unless he has her consent."

Judy looked swiftly at him, surprise in her face. Then she turned and walked back up the slope.

The driver was standing on the wheel hub, drinking from a bottle of whiskey tilted skyward. Jim followed her up the slope to where she stopped beside the driver, who looked at her, then turned to take another drink of whiskey.

"Driver, can't we cross?" she asked.

"No, ma'am."

"But you can if the women passengers give consent, can't you? That's in the rules, isn't it?"

The driver glared at her. "Who said so?"

Judith turned to Jim, standing a few feet away, and gestured to him. "He did."

The driver's gaze shuttled to Jim and contempt veiled his eyes. He was not an observant man, or else he would never have said what he said next. "Maybe that dude would like to take the stage across."

"Maybe I would," Jim answered quietly.

The driver glared at him and then swung heavily to the ground and walked over to him. "Looks easy, don't it?" he sneered.

"Doesn't look hard," Jim drawled.

"Well, it's hard enough that it ain't goin' to be done," the driver said.

"Let's take a vote on this," Jim suggested. "I don't savvy your company rules, driver, but in cases like this, most companies leave it up to the passengers when there's room for doubt. You know and I know that wash can be crossed. You've got a right to hold back in the interests of the passengers. But if the passengers say the word, it's up to you to cross." He turned and called to the whiskey drummer, who had not got out of the stage. When he came up to them, Jim said, "Want to risk the crossin'?"

"Sure," the drummer said promptly. "It's better than sleeping in that piano box all night."

Jim turned to the driver. "It's all right with the lady and it's all right with me. So we cross, fella'."

"Do we now?" the driver said coldly. "We

damn well don't.'' He laughed and walked over to the side of the rough road and from within a clump of *chamiso* he dragged out a brown jug. "I got a date with this little lady,'' he drawled, grinning. "I left her here last trip. She's honin' for a little attention. So you three just make yourselves right comfortable, because we ain't leavin' till that wash is runnin' only six inches of water.''

Jim dropped his cigar and walked over to the driver. "You aim to get up there in the box, or do you want to be tucked up there?''

The tone of his voice warned the driver. He put the jug down and squared away and said, "Mister, you and all your kin couldn't put me up there.''

"Get up there!'' Jim said harshly.

"Put me up there!''

Jim took a step forward and instantly the driver's hand streaked for his gun. Jim cut down with the edge of his hand, and it met the driver's wrist as his hand swept up. The gun somersaulted out of leather and fell into the dust. For one moment, the driver hesitated, bewildered almost, and then with a curse he caved.

Grumbling, the man climbed up into the box. But Jim was taking no chances. He hoisted himself up beside him. But before he did, he walked over to the girl.

"There's still light enough to cross,'' he told her. "Do you want to?''

"Yes.''

Jim looked out at the water. The wash was wide, racing dangerously, but there were no logs coming down. He said quietly. "Do you mind gettin' wet?''

"Of course not.''

Jim explained his scheme. The only danger was that the stage might be overturned in the flood. Therefore, she and the whiskey drummer were to stand on the upstream door, hands on the toprail, and lean out over the water, their bodies thus serving as a counter-balance to the force of the flood. When he was finished, Judy said, "You must have done this before, then?"

"I've ridden a lot of stages in my day," was Jim's noncommittal answer.

They climbed back to the stage and, when everything was ready, at Jim's command, the driver gathered the ribbons in his hand, kicked off the brake and let the stage roll down the slope.

The teams took to the water reluctantly and the driver had to use the whip. They began to swim, turning downstream and then, with a lurch, the coach left solid ground. It tipped precariously and the whiskey drummer let out a frightened curse. But it righted itself and swung downstream, sideways.

Jim stood up now, his face tense. The stream was swift, the harness heavy, but the horses were working.

They were more than halfway across when Jim felt the driver give a sudden start beside him. Suddenly, the man lurched up, dropping the reins, and the line of horses swung downstream again. From a scabbard inside his waist he had drawn a knife. Gripping it tightly he lunged at Jim. Jim leaped back atop the coach. It was too late to draw his gun. Plunging in he snatched the driver's wrist.

Somehow, out of the tail of his eye, Jim caught a glimpse of the passengers in the coach as he struggled with the driver. The drummer's face was pasty white. Judy Elliot's face was tense.

"If it goes over, jump clear!" Jim called as he rolled over, pinning the driver beneath him. But even as he spoke, the coach took a swift dive on its nose, then righted itself and once more floated. With a loose baggage strap Jim tied the driver. It was an easy matter then to let the coach swing around and guide the horses to the bank. When the leaders got their feet on solid ground, the race was won. Jim rested the teams in the water a few moments and then, with his eyes still on the driver, he cracked his whip over their heads and forced them up the steep bank and onto dry ground.

Dismounting, he climbed down. Judy was already on the ground and, with courtesy reversed, was helping the shaking whiskey drummer to the ground. There was excitement in her blue eyes as she turned to Jim and brushed a strand of her sleek chestnut hair off her cheek.

"That was wonderful," she said.

Jim grinned. "That'll cut one night off your time to the Coast, anyway, miss." And he turned to the whiskey drummer. "Help me sling the driver in the boot, will you?"

Together they contrived to put the inert form of the driver, hands and feet bound, into the rear boot. The girl came to Jim then.

"I'm not going to the Coast," she said, looking at him.

"I thought maybe I should tell you. This next town is my stop—Ft. Kendall."

Jim's grin broadened a little. "That's where I'm goin' to, Miss." He paused. "Maybe we'll see somethin' of each other."

"Perhaps," Judy said, color crawling into her face. "I'll be at the Army post." She hesitated, and then said softly. "You see, I'm going out there to get married. That's the reason I'm in a hurry.''

Jim blushed now too, and then he laughed softly. "Then I reckon I take that back, miss.'' And she laughed too.

Dusk had fallen now. The whiskey drummer had the inside of the stage to himself, for Judy, her wet feet wrapped in a dirty buffalo robe, rode on top with Jim.

The road to Fort Kendall ribboned down off a ridge into the main street which was now lighted against the early evening. Fort Kendall, the town, thrived in the shadow of Fort Kendall, the army post, two miles to the north. Beef drives for army contracts, freighting, stores and supplies all contributed to the prosperity of the town which flanked a wide and dusty main street. Even at night its traffic was unabated. Bullwhackers, mule-skinners, gamblers and punchers mingled with the army men on its sidewalks and in its saloons.

Jim rolled the stage up in front of the express office and two hustlers leaped to unhitch the teams for the change of horses. Jim jumped down and helped Judy off the stage. She did not even pause to thank him as she ran past him into the arms of a tall army man. Jim turned away to climb up on top again and throw down the luggage. Judy's went first, handed down to the drummer, and then came his own.

Once on the ground again, he was turning back to free the driver when he felt a hand on his shoulder. He turned to confront Judy and her lieutenant, a tall, wide-shouldered man in trim army blue.

"I—I don't know your last name, Jim,'' Judy

began. "But this is my fiancé, Lieutenant George Harms."

"Cade's the name," Jim murmured and extended his hand.

Harms was blond, his smooth, almost arrogant face burned to a golden brown by the sun. Jim saw at a glance that he was one of those men who rode high wide and handsome all through life. Things were made easy for a man like that, and things that weren't—well, he was a big man and a good one and he could take care of them.

"I'm obliged, sir," he said to Jim, smiling a little. "Judy tells me you did a right royal job of drivin'—and taking care of the driver."

Jim made a deprecating gesture. "We all wanted to get through with it, I reckon."

"We hope to see you up at the post, sir, if your stay is long enough," Lieutenant Harms went on. And then, saluting, he turned and called an order to a trooper standing on the boardwalk.

Judy's luggage was loaded into an army ambulance; she was assisted in and they drove off. She waved goodbye, and Jim touched his hat brim, his eyes reflective.

Then he turned and went about his business of unloading the driver. He heard a voice say behind him:

"That's a plumb queer place for a stage driver." The voice was deep, commanding, Jim turned to confront a big man, his hands rammed in his pockets, regarding the stage. He wore twin sixguns crossed beneath a fancy waistcoat.

Jim looked at his heavy, slack-jowled face and immediately didn't like it. "Ain't it?" he said.

"It's so funny," the man went on, "I'd like to know how he got there."

"I'll tell you," the drummer began from beside Jim, but the big man cut in.

"No you won't, drummer. I'm talkin' to that other jasper." All the good nature had left the man's voice.

Jim paid no attention. He pulled the last ropes loose, then hoisted the driver out onto the road. He had to hold him up a minute, for the whiskey, the wetting, the bouncing and the beating were almost too much for the driver and he was still groggy.

Then Jim turned to the stranger. "Seems to me you're mighty curious about my affairs," he murmured.

"I ought to be," the man replied. "I'm the divisional superintendent of this stage line. Name's Max Raine, in case you want to check up."

Jim's face hardened a little. "Are you?" he murmured politely. "Well, that ought to give you the right to ask. Anywhere we can talk alone, Raine?"

Raine jerked his head toward a small building wedged between two stores. "There's my office."

Jim said to the driver, "You better come along too, fella'."

"He's taking the stage on through," Raine said curtly.

"Your mistake," Jim answered mildly. "He's comin' along with us."

The driver swore darkly. "You're damn right I am," he said. "Wait'll I tell Raine what happened."

Raine shrugged and went inside. The front of the building was given over to benches, the middle part behind the wicket to the storage of the freight. Behind them, in the rear, was a partitioned-off office.

Raine entered and sat down in the chair in front

of his desk. Jim lounged against the wall and the driver stood by Raine.

"Now let's have it," Raine said curtly.

"I got held up by a wet arroyo over east," the driver began. "This *hombre* and a woman and that whiskey drummer out there wanted to cross. I wouldn't have any of it. It was dangerous. When I objected, he beat me up, tied me up and threw me in the back boot and then crossed the stage." He looked evilly at Jim. "I suppose you'll try to dodge that, mister."

Jim shrugged. "He could have crossed himself. Instead of that, he wanted to camp there tonight and fill his skin with whiskey."

"That's no business of yours," Raine cut in coldly. "We'll discipline our own men, not leave it to strangers."

"Go ahead and discipline him, then," Jim drawled.

Raine's face flushed. He took the big cigar from his mouth and swung his feet to the floor. "I don't think I'll bother with you any longer," Raine murmured. "We got a sheriff in this county that knows what to do with gents like you."

"Sit down!" Jim whipped out. The iron in his voice was unmistakable. Raine settled back in his chair, his eyes wide.

"Now I'll talk," Jim said. "I'm Jim Cade and I've been sent out by the El Paso office to kick you out of here and take over the division, Raine. I was told to use my own judgment about the method I used in telling you, but after tonight, I won't bother. You're fired. Pack up your stuff and clear out of here now. Here's a letter from the General Manager of the line."

Raine read it and put it on the desk. "What've I done that I shouldn't?" he growled.

"What have you done you should have?" Jim countered coldly. "We've had more Indian raids in your division, Raine, than in all the others put together. We can't keep a herd of horses at a stage station for more than a week. We can't assure any shipper—not even the government—that the mail will get through."

"I got the toughest division in the country," Raine pointed out. "I've got Apaches, and even the government knows what they are."

"We've got Comanches and Kiowas over east," Jim said coldly. "It doesn't happen there." He shook his head. "You're through, Raine. You haven't got an alibi that's worth a damn. If your men were good drivers, if they did their best, if they tried to make schedule, if they cared about their jobs and had some pride in them, I reckon it'd be different. But tonight was a good example of how your men work for you. They don't." He looked up at the driver. "Draw your time and get out!"

Raine looked obliquely at his driver and then back at Jim. Suddenly, he laughed, a little ruefully, and got up. "All right, Cade. I know when I'm licked. I done the best I could, but it wasn't good enough." He extended his hand. "No hard feelings."

"No," Jim said. He put out his hand and Raine grasped it. Suddenly, the driver exploded into action. He took a long swing at Jim's head.

Jim, with his right hand held in the vise of Raine's grip, could not protect himself. But he could duck, and he did, letting the blow catch him on the shoulder. It sent him crashing against the wall. He caught himself, half stumbling, and fell to his knees. Twisting around, his hand falling to his gun, he looked up at Raine—and into the barrel of a Colt .44.

"Well, well," Raine drawled. "So you don't like the way we do business, eh? Abe, get that gun." The driver took Jim's gun.

"Let's see," Raine drawled. "I don't recollect that he told Harms' girl his business here, did he, Abe?"

"Not that I heard," Abe said.

"Then it won't be hard to spread the story that he bought a pony and rode on through because he couldn't get a seat in the stage." He turned to Jim, smiling, "You've got too long a nose, fella. We're doin' nicely without you."

A new voice broke in, a voice from the rear door, "And I'd do right nicely without you, Raine."

Jim's gaze shuttled past Raine to the door. There, just inside it, stood the wiriest, brownest, driest little man that he had ever seen. He was dressed in buckskin and moccasins and he held a sixgun in his hand.

"Drop those irons!" he ordered curtly. Raine did so, along with Abe. They both turned slowly to identify this man. "Now walk over there face to the wall where I can get a good bead on your backs."

Raine's face was glistening with sweat. "My God, Poke. You can't do that!"

"But you can, eh?" the little man sneered. "You'll see if I can't. Now walk over there."

Jim had the sudden conviction that Poke meant to do exactly what he said. "Wait a minute!" he broke in quickly. "They're scared enough, Poke. Let 'em go."

"Let 'em go!" Poke exclaimed. "Why, hell, man, they was goin' to beef you."

"Let 'em go," Jim repeated. "The stage company will make more trouble for you than they're worth."

Poke considered this a moment, his leathery old face screwed up with thought. "Maybe you're right," he drawled. "But if I catch them two coyotes in this town after two minutes is up, I'll spread the word what they aimed to do. And a lynch mob ain't a pretty thing to watch." To Raine and Abe he said, "Drag it!"

Raine dived for the back door, Abe on his heels. When they were gone, Jim regarded the man before him, grinned and put out his hand.

"Name's Cade, and I reckon you know just about how glad I was to see you. Much obliged. But just how did you know I was in this jam?"

"Easy," Poke said, and spat. "When you rolled that stage in, I could tell you wasn't no dude, like you're dressed for. Then I seen Abe in the rear boot, the water marks on the stage and I heard what you said to Raine. Puttin' all those together, I figured there'd be trouble, so I just snuck down the alley here and listened at the back door. Shootin's too good for Raine, though."

"Why?"

"Why?" Poke echoed, looking at Jim queerly. "Well, for one thing, I heard you mention that more horses had been stole off the stage stations in this division here than any division on your line."

"That's right."

"Funny thing, but across the Border Mexes are buyin' mighty fine horses for damn little money.

Some of them broncs has even got harness galls on
'em.''

"But the Apaches steal them."

"Sure," Poke said. "They steal 'em and they
get money for 'em. But did you ever see an
Apache that had use for money? They don't use
the money. Somebody does."

"Raine?"

"I ain't sayin'."

"There've been massacres on this line too,"
Jim said slowly. "Raine too?"

"I ain't sayin'. Neither is the army. If it could
be proved, Raine'd be a dead man."

Jim looked thoughtfully at Poke. "He's a renegade white, then?"

"He ain't white, but he's plenty renegade."

Just then the drummer burst into the office.
"Who's the manager here?"

"I am," Jim said.

"Well, that stage has been loaded and waitin'
for fifteen minutes. Where's the driver?"

Jim looked at Poke. "Can you find me one?"

Poke nodded and walked on past him. Five
minutes later, the San Francisco bound stage rolled
out of Fort Kendall with a capable driver at the
ribbons, and a full passenger list inside and on top.

It was just getting light when Jim was awakened at
his room at the hotel by a pounding on his door.
He reached for his gun on the table, then got out
of bed, pulled on his pants and went to the door.

"Who is it?" he asked in a low voice.

"Cade, I've got some news for you."

Jim unlocked the door and a dirty, amiable looking cowpuncher stepped into the room. "You're
the new stage line super, ain't you? Well, your

stage was caught by the Apaches out west here. Every livin' soul in it was massacred and robbed and scalped. They burned the stage, took the mail and horses and disappeared.''

"You see it?" Jim answered in a low voice.

"I found it," the driver said. "It wasn't purty, either. I'm on my way to tell the army now. I thought you'd ought to know."

"Wait a minute," Jim said. "I'll be with you."

He dressed in worn levis and blue shirt, strapped a gun on his hip, then went out with the messenger. He got a horse at the livery stable, borrowed a saddle and together they headed for the Fort.

Fort Kendall was just waking up for the day when they got there. It was a large fort, with only the munitions storehouse enclosed by a stockade. The parade grounds were spacious, and off to one side of it, under a few tall lodgepole pines, were the cottages of the commandant and his staff.

It was for these houses the messenger headed. They were shown by a Mexican maid into a small room reflecting a military neatness even in the distribution of the Eastern furniture. Minutes later, Major Morse came in and introduced himself. He was a man of middle stature with a kindly, firm face, and it was to Cade he listened as Jim identified himself and offered a letter of introduction from the commandant at Fort Carson.

Major Morse glanced at it and said, "Oh, yes. I've had orders to co-operate with you in any way possible, Cade."

"And I reckon it'll begin right now," Jim said, and told him of the massacre. Major Morse's face took on a stony look as Jim finished. Jim mentioned nothing concerning Raine, for he wanted to talk to Poke first. When Major Morse had heard him out, he sent the puncher to summon an adjutant, and then turned to Jim and invited him to breakfast.

When Jim walked into the dining room, the first person he saw was Judy Elliot. They looked at each other, both surprised.

"He's the man, Uncle Boyd, who drove the stage through!" Judy explained.

Major Morse looked at Jim with an added respect. Jim was seated and the Mexican maid served breakfast. He ate and let Major Morse tell Judy what had happened.

She listened to the story with wide-eyed wonder, and when he was finished, she shivered a little. Jim knew she was thinking that it was the same stage which she had left in Fort Kendall last night.

"But what will you do, Uncle Boyd?" she asked finally.

"I'm going to give that man of yours a chance to show his mettle again," the Major answered.

Judy flushed a little and looked obliquely at Jim, whose face was impassive.

"Lieutenant Harms," the Major went on grimly, "will take a detail, as many townsmen as he needs and as many scouts as he wants, and he'll come back here with the accounts squared."

After breakfast, Jim parted from Judy with a handshake and brief thanks, and he and the Major went to the headquarters building.

Lieutenant Harms was already there waiting, and he smiled at Jim. Morse gave him his orders, adding, "If I were in your place, Lieutenant, I would take Poke Harris as scout. He's fought these Apaches so long he thinks like one himself."

"My intentions, exactly, Major."

"Good luck, Lieutenant."

Harms saluted and he and Jim went out. In front of the barracks, a platoon of cavalry troopers were at ease beside their horses. Poke Harris, in filthy buckskin, sat a little way apart, smoking a cigarette. His pack consisted of a thin saddle roll behind the cantle and nothing else, in contrast to the bulky packs of the cavalry men. Five heavily loaded pack horses were included in the group.

"You aim to travel that heavy, Lieutenant?" Poke asked. His eyes settled on Jim for one moment, and they were friendly. Then they shifted to Harms.

"The men have got to eat, Poke," Harms said easily.

"Not if they're runnin' down Apaches, they don't. They can't."

Harms laughed good-naturedly. "I've heard about your convictions in Indian fighting, Poke. You show us where the Apaches are. We'll do the rest."

"Not with twenty-five men," Poke said stubbornly. "If you aim to travel this way, you'd better call out a company."

Harms face lost a little of its good nature. "You're the scout, Poke. That's all the help I'll ask from you."

Helplessly, Poke shrugged and turned to his horse. Harms gave the order to mount and they trotted smartly across the parade grounds. Passing the major's house, Judy, on the porch, waved to them, and Harms saluted gravely in reply. He was a handsome figure on his chestnut gelding, and Jim looked from him to Judy, understanding her pride in him. In spite of himself, Jim could not help feeling a little jealous of Harms.

Off the military grounds, Harms directed the

platoon west across the sage flats that would eventually take them to the road.

It was here that Poke pulled his horse in toward Harms and said, "I reckon I'll drop in to town and catch up with you, Harms. I fergot tobacco." An hour later, he joined them again and fell in without speaking.

The place where the stage was stopped was a narrow foothills canyon of the timbered Pima range. They reached the place at noon, and even at that hour it was dark and somehow sinister looking. Sergeant Clay, in the van, pulled up and pointed down into the canyon where the charred skeleton of the stage lay in a rocky stream bed. The platoon filed down into the canyon.

Closer now, the story was all too eloquent. Four bodies, dragged under a piñon, had all been scalped. Across the stream and in the water were five more bodies. Every passenger had been scalped first and then shot.

Looking at it, the men turned sick, but Harms, resolutely ordered them to go ahead and dismount.

"Wait," Poke said quietly. "I'd like a look at the ground before it's tromped up."

Harms let him go ahead. Poke's examination was swift, expert, and as soon as he found what he wanted, he motioned them to come on. Harms detailed a burial squad, which was soon busy. Poke squatted on his haunches, smoking, under a tree.

Jim rode up to him, dismounted and looked over the ground. His examination was only a shade less thorough and swift than Poke's and then he came over and sat beside the Indian scout.

"How many'd you count?" Poke asked.

"Fourteen Indians," Jim murmured.

"What else?"

Jim sifted gravel through his fingers for a moment before he answered obliquely. "Did you ever know an Apache to wear cow boots?"

"No."

"Then fourteen Indians and one white."

Poke nodded gravely. "Don't tell Harms. It'll just make him that much more bullheaded."

He regarded Jim now with a look in which there was a respect added to his friendliness. Harms came over and said, "How big was the raiding party, Poke?"

"Fourteen."

Harms nodded. "Good. Then I can leave ten of my men to this burial detail and we can get along with the job."

Poke's face showed he was about to protest, for that left just fifteen men. "Still travelin' heavy?" he asked.

Harms nodded. Poke spat and looked away.

The lieutenant called out his orders, which were that ten men, under Corporal Wilson, were to attend to the burials and then go back to the Fort. The others were to mount immediately.

Poke went on ahead, Jim riding with him. The trail was plain, with no attempt at concealment. The Apaches, after their fashion, were driving a large remuda of horses which the stage broncs swelled. They were traveling hard and certainly toward the south, angling up into the foothills. At dusk, Harms gave the order to camp.

Poke said quietly, "Let me get this straight, Harms. Just how do you want to fight these Apaches?"

"Why, they'll hole up eventually and we'll smoke 'em out."

"Listen," Poke said patiently. "Do you know how Apaches fight? They travel with nothing but muskets, ball and powder, a handful of jerky, a geestring and a remuda. When they wear a horse down, they cut his throat and shift to another horse. Travelin' at this rate, stoppin' for grub and sleep, you'll hit their camp just when they want you to—in about three days. They'll have every buck in the country, from fifteen to fifty, waitin' for us. It'll be another massacre."

"What do you want us to do?" Harms asked coldly, anger creeping into his voice.

"Ride!" Poke said curtly. "Dump your blankets, and travel with nothin' but guns and hardtack. Ride day and night and you got a chance to cut 'em off before they reach the Nations Peak country."

"I'm running this party," Harms said slowly. "I hope they lead us to their camp. It'll be a chance to wipe out all those dogs."

"Yeah, it'll be a chance," Poke conceded drily, turning away.

Two days later, they had worked deep into the Nations Peak country, a wild, high plateau with the mountain range ahead of them. It was a small range, but high and desolate. The men were uneasy, for this was a country of evil reputation. The army had been in here before in pursuit of Apaches, but each time it was with a full company.

Jim noticed that Poke had kept utterly silent these last two days. He and Harms had arrived at a truce.

Their approach could not help but have been known to the Apaches, but so far there were no signs of them. The raiders' trail lay straight for the peaks.

It was mid morning when the troopers reached the abrupt foothills of the Nations. Harms called a halt and then turned to Poke. "Pick the trail, Poke."

"Not me," Poke said mildly.

Harms stared at him. "You mean you're not going on?"

"Not unless I'm carried," Poke said. "And the man that carries me has got to shoot me. Harms, you've made a lot of mistakes this trip, but you've made two that are real ones. In the first place, you made the mistake of crossin' the flat in daylight. Even a blind Apache could see you. And now you aim to start into that Malpais so you'll have to camp here tonight."

"But why are they mistakes?" Harms asked.

Poke shrugged. "I ain't got much hair, left, but I'd rather see it on my head than hangin' from one of those Apaches' geestrings."

Harms was silent for a moment, then his gaze shuttled to Jim. "You feel that way about it too, Cade?"

"Pretty close," Jim murmured.

"You understand, do you, that I'm in command of this detail. When you agreed to come, it was with the understanding that I gave the orders. My orders are that you stay with us."

Jim reined his horse over close to Harms. "Lieutenant," he drawled, "I'm a plain citizen. I've never took army pay and don't aim to. And seein' as how that's the way it is, I'd like to see you make me go on with you."

Harms was surprised at the tone in Jim's voice, and Jim was surprised himself. But the insufferable conceit of this soldier and his attitude toward Poke had angered him beyond his knowing.

"I might have expected this from a stage agent," Harms sneered, looking at Poke, "but I hardly expected it from a government scout."

"Ex-government scout," Poke said.

"True," Harms said drily. "Your services with the army are ended, Poke."

"That bein' the case," Poke said slowly, after he had spat, "I won't trouble you no further, Harms. Take a look at the sun, though, before you camp tonight. It's likely the last time you'll see it."

Wheeling his horse, he turned with Jim back over the trail they had just come over. When, half an hour later, they looked back, they saw no sign of Harms and the troopers.

"I hate that," Jim said finally, reluctantly. "We should have gunwhipped Harms and brought those boys out."

"Not a chance," Poke said bitterly. "They'd have fought for him, son."

"But they're going to their death!"

"Look here!" Poke burst out suddenly, turning to Jim. "I hate this as much as you do, Cade. Them troopers are good lads and they got to obey orders, even if they do come from a damn fool."

Jim pulled up his horse, sighing with relief. "That's the way I feel about it, Poke. Let's go back—even if we are fools."

"I got a better plan than that," Poke said. "Come on."

He did not turn back. Instead, he turned off the trail north across the long mesa. No amount of questioning could make him tell Jim what was

afoot. At dusk, they sloped down off the mesa to a
dry stream bed and followed it north until they
came to a log shack set deep in a cottonwood
thicket. The dirt roof had partially fallen in, but a
thin streamer of smoke was issuing from the pipe.
There were two horses staked out in the tall grass
in front of the shack.

At a halloo from Poke a rough looking puncher
emerged cautiously from the cabin, a rifle in his
hands. Poke and Jim rode up and dismounted.

"Get the stuff all right, Ferg?" Poke asked.

"It's in the shack," Ferg said. The three of
them went into the shack. There, stacked in a
corner were two ten gallon kegs.

Poke paid him off in gold coins and the man
wasted no time in getting saddled. He waved to
them, wished them good luck, and then rode off.
He left his pack horse.

Poke chuckled at the sight of him riding away.
"He don't like this country," Poke drawled. "This
used to be his shack before the Apaches drove him
out."

Jim motioned with his head toward the shack.
"What'd he bring?"

"Somethin' I ordered," Poke drawled. "Remember when I rode into town the mornin' we left
Kendall?" When Jim nodded, Poke continued,
"Well, that's when I ordered. You see, I had
Harms figured out pretty good. I knowed the 'Paches
would never have raided that stage unless they was
headed to hole up over here. And I knowed Harms
wouldn't hurry to cut 'em off. So I brought my
own medicine."

"What?"

"Whiskey."

Jim looked at him and Poke accepted his stare.

Without speaking they both understood what Poke was planning.

"It's risky," Poke said gently. "You want to try it?"

Jim nodded. "Won't they guess why you brought it?"

"Let 'em," Poke said curtly. "It won't keep 'em from drinkin' it." He looked strangely at Jim. "You see," he said quietly, "I got a powerful hankerin' to see the inside of that Apache camp. I think I might find somethin' there that would be considerably interestin' to both of us."

It was midnight when they set out with the Fergusson pack horse loaded down with the two kegs of whiskey. By daylight, they were well into the twisting mountain trails of the Nations Peak. Neither of them talked much, for they both knew they had a fifty-fifty chance of coming out of this alive.

Early in the morning, as if guessing Jim's thoughts, Poke said. "Old Chief Thunder Hand will be mighty happy when he lays hands on me. Him and me have met before. He's got a standin' offer of a brand new army rifle for the buck that brings me to him alive."

"Torture?"

"Yeah."

They nooned by a small trickle of water which ran through the sparse timber, and ate jerky. Afterwards, while Poke was tightening the pack rope Jim did something which he had been contemplating all morning. He took off his gunbelt and rammed his gun down the inside of his boot next his leg. In his other boot, he put his knife, a thin, flat bowie.

Along toward the middle of the afternoon, Poke

began to look worried. Aloud, he wondered if the Apaches were so off their guard that they did not have lookouts stationed. It would spoil their plans.

Suddenly a shot cracked out and Poke's horse pitched to its knees. Only by the quickest of movements was Poke able to clear the saddle before the horse rolled. Before Jim could rein up, there were four figures on the trail ahead. He hoisted his hands and the four Apaches ran at a dog trot down the trail.

This was the first good look he had ever had of an Apache and he understood now why they were so feared. These men were not overtall, but they were rawhide lean and hard as iron. Their faces, with the thin nose and flat cheekbones were the cruelest he had ever seen on Indians.

The leader approached Poke on the run and then stopped suddenly. He had an army musket in his hand. The other three ran up to Jim, covering him with similar muskets. Then the Indian in front of Poke began to talk rapidly to his companion and Poke cut in with a sentence of Apache.

"What'd you tell 'em?" Jim asked.

"I told them they had better not hurt us and that they'd better run because the army was here and had taken their camp. The buck laughed and said they had taken the army. Then I told him he was mistaken because I had orders to bring the fire water for the army to celebrate."

"Did they know you?"

The conversation ceased then, for the Apaches dragged Jim off his horse. He and Poke were commanded to walk ahead, after their rifles were seized. Ahead, the Apaches had some horses waiting. They mounted, and Jim and Poke were made to walk. At sunset, the order was reversed, and Jim and Poke were tied on the Apache ponies while the Apaches walked. They were heading into timber now, angling up the mountainside.

Several hours past dark, they saw a light ahead in the trees. One of the Apaches shouted and received an answer.

Then they were led into a large clearing. One glance told Jim that the worst would happen. One long huge fire had been built and posts had been placed in the ground all around it. And to these posts, each trooper was tied.

The troopers were on their knees, back to the fire, their hands laced with thongs to the post. The look of despair in their faces made Jim heartsick. They did not even greet him as the Apaches, a howling insane mob now, pulled them off their horses and bound them in a manner similar to the others.

The Apaches now seemed to be arguing over by the whiskey. Even the drum beater, whose activity Jim and Poke's entry had interrupted, had left his post to join his brothers. Jim was tied only a few feet from Harms, whose pale face was set in a hopeless cast. He regarded Jim with a look of bitterness.

Poke was listening carefully to the talk of the bucks.

"What are they sayin', Poke," Jim asked.

"Arguin' over the booze. Seems like Thunder Hand ain't here and neither is the White Friend." He looked meaningly at Jim. "The more level-headed of the bucks want to save the booze until they get here." He turned back and listened some more, then said, "There's a war party over the peaks here. Thunder Hand is with them. Seems like they've sent a messenger over to him and the

White Friend to tell them to leave the war party and come in a hurry.''

''Why?''

''So they can fry us,'' Poke said quietly. He looked over at Harms now and said mildly, ''Satisfied, Lieutenant?''

The shouting of the bucks now made speech impossible. Apparently, the faction which favored breaking open the kegs was in the majority, for the whiskey was brought out into the clear and the soldiers' packs were raided for the tincups. Several of the braves, scowling mightily, took no part in the drinking.

Poke watched it all with calm eye. ''They got a treat comin','' he observed mildly. ''You see, it really ain't whiskey. It's grain alcohol and tobacco. Ferg knows the army sutler and he got the alcohol. Watch out, because they'll get pretty wild.''

''Are you tied tight?'' Jim asked softly.

''I ain't had a chance to find out. When they get to drinkin' it'll be time enough. Watch out for the sober ones, because they'll watch us.''

Poke's predictions turned out to be accurate. The whiskey inflamed passions were already running high. The drummer started to beat on the huge skin-headed drum and a dance began. Soon, the whole camp, except for a handful of the most responsible bucks, joined in.

This was the time to work, Jim knew. They seemed to want to let Poke and himself alone, perhaps afraid of the wrath of Thunder Hand, who had always wanted this old white man.

His own bonds, Jim found, were not tied very well. The excitement of the night had made his captors a little careless. But it was rawhide he was tied with, and he pulled silently till he felt a warm wash of blood over his wrists. Still his bonds did not stretch, although he had worked them loose enough so that he could slide his wrists down the tree to which he was bound. He did so until he could touch his boots with numbed fingers. Kneeling in a tortuous position now, he worked slowly and doggedly at his boot.

Inching his wet fingers inside the top of the boot, he could reach the knife handle, but it was wedged solidly against his leg. It took fifteen minutes of two-fingered fumbling to work it loose.

The dance was a wild fury now. Already, some of the bucks were lying on the ground, dead drunk, for this was a fire water of high potency. The sober bucks had their hands full.

And all the time Jim was working frantically. When the bonds on his wrists finally parted, he picked up the knife and sawed at the thongs around his ankles. His next move was to pull out the gun rammed in his boot, his arms still behind him.

Then he waited, watching. A violent quarrel started up at the far end of the fire and every buck in the camp seemed to join in.

It was then that Jim heard Poke murmur, "Do it now, boy."

Jim ducked around the tree and knelt behind Poke. In a moment, Poke's thongs were cut. Without waiting for a word, Poke leaped for the trooper's guns which were stacked up by a wickiup. At the same time, one of the sober Apaches saw them. He leaped for the guns, and Jim shot. The buck went down and the camp fell silent.

Not an Apache in that camp was so drunk but what he realized his mistake. They had been dancing with the old weapons, the tomahawk and the knife, leaving the firearms unguarded. Poke knelt over the firearms and picked up two six-guns.

"Put your knife in my teeth," he said quickly, "then run for it."

"But—"

"I know," Poke said. "Get that renegade white. I can take care of this." The only pass in these peaks lies to the south. Now—the knife."

Jim slipped the knife in Poke's teeth and Poke, a gun in each hand, rose and walked toward the Apaches. Jim waited no more. He knew if any man could make a bluff work, Poke could.

He ran for the horses corraled outside the clearing. Once there, he did not take time to saddle, but led one of the Apache ponies outside the stake corral and closed the entrance. Then he mounted, and headed off into the night.

He was less than a minute away from the camp when he heard the spatter of gunfire and the yelling of the Indians. He smiled thinly, content, for he knew that Poke had done it. In the next fifteen minutes, not an Apache would be left alive in that camp. It was a hard country, and troopers do not forget.

At daylight, he was able to pick up the trail that led to the pass, and by midmorning he was approaching the pass itself. It was little more than a foot trail twisting up through the boulder fields. Later, it left these and started up the almost sheer side of a peak. There was room on the trail for a single horse, no more.

It was here in a little rincon that Jim tied his pony, out of sight. He walked from there, watching the trail carefully, searching for the right place. Where the sheer wall gave way a little there was a deep pocket eroded by the wind. It could shelter a man and screen him from sight of the trail, although he was so close to it he could have touched a man passing.

Jim considered the place of concealment a long time. He could lie in wait here. If only Thunder Hand and the Renegade White came along, he could take care of them. But if the Apache war party came, he would be sure to be discovered.

He crawled into the little pocket and wedged himself in a squatting position to wait. As he let the silence of the hot noon settle around him, he began to grow sleepy. Soon, it took all his strength to fight the sleep and weariness that was overtaking him. Minutes later, then, he didn't even care. Nothing in the world would be important enough to keep him from sleeping, he thought.

Suddenly, a sound pounded into his consciousness and he listened idly, sleepily. And then, like a flash of lightning, it came to him. Someone was coming. With a jerk, he was wide awake.

He waited. If there were two of them, he would have to get rid of one, and quickly. He drew his gun, holding his breath. The noise of horses came closer.

Then he saw a horse's head pass him, then the withers and then he saw the thigh of a naked Indian. He shoved himself out from the wall, kicking.

Thunder Hand only got a glimpse of him before the impact. The old Indian moved like an attacking animal. He whirled, grabbed Jim's boot and held to it as he caromed out of the saddle.

The horse bolted and Jim was pulled out onto the trail. Thunder Hand, lying on his back, teetered for one moment on the edge of the trail and then rolled over. Jim braced himself against the pull, dropping his gun, clawing at the rock. Then the weight of the Apache yanked and he felt himself sliding. Suddenly, something gave way. He felt his boot slip off, and a high keening wail rose on the still air.

Jim looked up then—and into the smiling features of Max Raine, mounted on an Indian pony, a gun trained on him.

"That was all right—but clumsy," Raine said coldly. He laughed. "Would you be interested to know that your gun is down there with Thunder Hand?"

Jim, still sprawled on his belly, moved his hand down to his thigh which rested on a hard object he thought was the gun. It was Thunder Hand's tomahawk.

A tomahawk against a gun, Jim thought desperately. His hand grasped the handle of the tomahawk and he groaned softly.

"You got me, Raine," he said quietly. "I think my legs broke. I can't move.

"Good," Raine said, cocking his gun with a distinct click. "You'll make a good target." He sighted along his gun.

Jim rolled over just as the gun thundered. He felt a hot sear across his back, but he came to his knees and threw the tomahawk. It went straight as an arrow past the still leveled gun and caught Raine in the shoulder. He clawed at it with his gun hand, dropping the gun to the trail.

Jim made a dive for it between the pony's legs and the pony reared. Jim fell on his face, expecting the horse to come down on him, but at the same time he saw the gun slide off the trail.

It all happened fast then. Between the horse's

hind legs, Jim saw Raine slope off onto the trail. The horse gave a savage whistle and came down on all fours, on top of Jim, but missing him. Then he stampeded down the trail, stepping over Jim with the agility of a mountain pony.

Raine was on his hands and knees now and Jim rose to face him. They were both weaponless, Jim thought, until he saw that Raine had the tomahawk in his hand.

They stood erect, watching each other. Then Raine smiled and took a step forward. Jim leaped. His hand grasped Raine's wrist just at the peak of his down-swing and their bodies met in savage collision. They stood locked that way for ten full seconds, and then Raine's arm began to bend back. Panting, grunting, he fought to keep steady, but when he saw he was losing, he opened his hand and the tomahawk fell to the trail and skidded overside. But slowly, Jim knew, he was being forced to the outer edge of the trail where Raine could kick him off. In desperation, he resolved on a trick.

He suddenly relaxed, letting himself fall to the ground on his back. It caught Raine, who had been braced against the wall, unawares. He stumbled, tripped and sprawled on his hands and then Jim rolled to strike savagely with his left hand. The hook caught Raine in the back of the ear.

For one brief instant he balanced on the edge of the trail, then sagged over. He skidded off the cliff without a sound.

Jim lay on his face, his breath gagging with the labor of his breathing. When he had caught his wind once more, he pulled himself to the edge of the cliff. Far, far, below, almost side by side, the two bodies were sprawled.

Poke watched for two days, squatted against the stone side of the stables. He had seen many things from this place. He had seen Harms report to the Major, had seen the Major shake hands with him, and last night, he had seen Harms in the swing with Judy.

He knew the story Harms had told the Major and Judy because Judy had asked him to tell her more complete details. She had even asked Poke, her face sad and disillusioned, why Jim Cade had run away that night at the Apache camp.

At noon on the second day, Poke saw a weary horseman turn into the parade grounds. Poke was on his feet and running. He met Jim in the middle of the grounds and took the reins of his horse. Jim's face was haggard, unshaven, but grim no longer.

Major Morse came out. There was no sympathy in his face and Jim wondered wearily what was the matter.

"Now," Poke said slowly, "I ain't been asked to give my report of what happened. I just got patted on the back for thinkin' to lug whiskey to them Apaches. I'd like to hear your report first, Harms. Your report of Cade."

"He came into camp with you. You were seized and tied," Harms said coldly. "I didn't see any more until you and Cade made a run for the guns. Evidently they hadn't tied you securely and you broke loose. But instead of waiting to help you, Cade, like a coward, ran off and left Poke to free us singlehanded."

"That's your story?" Poke asked mildly, and Harms nodded.

Poke turned. "Where you been, Jim?"

Slowly, Jim told his story of the fight with Thunder Hand and Raine.

"Raine?" the Major interrupted. "You mean the stage agent?"

Then it was that the whole story came out. Poke told of how Harms had bull-headedly led the whole platoon into a death trap, and how he and Jim had refused to go. Poke didn't mince words. He laid the blame for the capture directly at the feet of Harms. He told of Jim's reluctance to leave the troopers to a fate which meant certain death.

"At every step," Poke told Major Morse grimly, "Harms was only thinkin' of the glory he could rake in. He didn't think of his men. He didn't take the advice of an Indian fighter and he didn't use the little sense the Lord give him. He may be a good soldier, Major Morse, but you take the regulations away from him and he couldn't fight flies."

"That's a hard accusation," Morse said sternly. "I don't think it's up to you to criticize."

"Did you hear me open my mouth when Harms gave you his report?"

"No."

"And I didn't open it until he started to run down the man who saved the whole platoon, me and him included, and then, on top of that, settled the Apache trouble in this section for good." Poke looked at the lot of them and then spat. He said to the Major: "You want my resignation? You'll get it. Damned if I'll work for a blow-hard lieutenant that not only ain't got any brains, but ain't got any gratitude either."

Harms' face was the color of brick. "I—I didn't know," he said.

"Of course you didn't. You don't know a damn thing," Poke said calmly.

Harms bowed and saluted, then stepped off the porch. Poke glared at him, then swung to face Judy. "If you come out here to marry him, Miss Judy, you ain't the girl I first took you for."

Judy was blushing, but her chin was up, a proud look in her face. "If you'd overheard just a little bit more, Poke, you'd know that George and I have been arguing for two days."

"About what?"

"About—about Jim Cade." She looked swiftly at Jim and then back at the Major. "Haven't we, Uncle Boyd?"

Major Morse smiled broadly and winked at Poke. "I've got some mighty old whiskey in the house, Poke. Let's drink to the damnation of the Apaches."

"And to blowhard lieutenants, too," Poke added. He followed Morse inside.

Once inside, Poke said, "Is what Judy said true? Did she stick up for him?"

"She did. Against me and against Lieutenant Harms, too."

"But why?"

Morse raised a finger and pointed to the front window. Framed in it were Judy and Jim sitting in the swing.

"It seems," the Major drawled, "that Judy is more interested in the stage business than the army."

Poke looked and nodded. "For good?"

"If Jim isn't a fool, it's for good," the Major said, smiling.

Hideout

He put his pistol away and tried not to look at his dead horse as he fumbled with numbed hands in an effort to get the saddle clear before it was drifted over. The wind boiled across the snow and beat his eyes shut, so that when he straightened into the full force of it, hefting his saddle, he was almost carried backward. He hung the saddle in a tree, a stubborn gesture of defiance that announced he would return, and afterwards he let the wind maul him down the timbered slope in the darkness, and he was a man without much hope.

Later, he found the stage road, found it by tripping and falling over the ridge of hard packed snow left by the stage wheels and now many inches under the rising white flood. Lying there on his face while the wind smoked across his back, his hand rested on the ridge made by the other wheel. It took a long time in his mind for the hint to turn into a hunch, and when it did and he lunged up into the weather again and saw the two dim parallel grooves sloping off across the timber, he shouted. For joy, maybe, or to remind himself that he had a voice.

The rest was just bulling it for another two dismal hours, and when the ground suddenly dipped and the timber fell away, and he faced a great unbroken sheet of snow which the wind was scouring tableflat, he knew it for the mountain meadow where Jim Hoskins and his wife ran the stage station.

It took him another forty-five minutes to reach Jim Hoskins' kitchen door, and when he threw it open and let the light blind him and the heat burn into his lungs, he was smiling, but not forgetting it.

"Why, Sam Johns, you big fool!" Mrs. Hoskins said. "What are you doing out in this?"

Sam leaned against the door and slowly picked the frost rime from his lashes, thankful for the door against his back. He saw Mrs. Hoskins, fat and bluff and not very jolly, her arms floured up to the elbows, standing over a pan of bread dough, and a strange woman, a girl, beside her.

"Getting lost, mostly," Sam said through stiff lips, and he smiled wryly. He tramped over to the big iron range, hoping his steps didn't drag too much, and put his back to it, facing the two women. They were waiting for him to talk, and he knew he wasn't going to, because a man doesn't talk about being afraid and knowing despair, and besides, it was fast fading now. He would have been a big man even without a mackinaw, and a week's beard stubble couldn't hide the pleasant gauntness of his long face. He said mildly, "That bread smells good," and looked at the girl, whose wide blue eyes showed a concern that made Sam uncomfortable.

"Land, I bet you haven't eaten since morning, have you?" Mrs. Hoskins asked.

Longer than that, Sam thought, and said, "That's what I meant."

That brought a smile from Mrs. Hoskins and the girl too. Sam's body drank in the heat while Mrs. Hoskins told the girl to finish kneading the bread while she got Sam a bite to eat. To Sam, she said, "You take off your things and tote some wood into the big room. The stage had to lay over and I can't do everything for all these people."

"Yes, ma'am," Sam said mildly. He pulled off his mackinaw, still bitterly cold, and he was grateful for the look of sympathy from the girl. She knew he wanted more than anything in the world right now to stand near the stove and let it thaw the memory of these last hours from his mind and body, instead of running errands for this busybody woman.

He took a load of pine chunks in his arms and stepped into the corridor. It was flanked by two tiny cubby holes of rooms, the doors hung with curtains, and it opened onto the big bare room in front, which was the dining and living room. Halfway down the corridor, Mrs. Hoskins said from behind him, "Sam."

Sam stopped, and the big woman came close to him and in a whisper that was far more penetrating than her ordinary voice said, "I want you to bust up that poker game in there, you hear? Her man" —she nodded toward the kitchen—"is losing all the money they'll be married on, and he won't quit. You send Jim out here to me, and you take his hand. Then when your supper's ready I'll call you, and maybe your going will bust it up. You hear?"

"All right," Sam said patiently, and went on into the big room, sick with hunger.

His entrance brought lazy greetings from bearded Jim Hoskins and Marky Wolf, the stage driver, two of the four at a poker game being played on upended suitcases close to the big fatbellied stove. Lying full length on a wall bench behind the stove was a thin little man in dapper city clothes, a scarf wound around his neck; and at his head, where she could watch over the shoulder of one of the players, sat a woman of the kind that earned her living in saloons and dance halls and frontier honkatonks.

She was a big bodied woman with a friendly, aging face, and she wore a heavy buffalo-skin coat over a dress that was too bright and too thin for either respectability or warmth.

She said, "Howdy," in a husky, friendly voice, and Sam smiled at her and dumped his wood by the stove. The little man behind it coughed softly and rhythmically and apologetically, a pitch below the wind which tore at the log eaves of the building.

Big Marky Wolf, his face more weather-reddened than usual, looked up from his cards long enough to drawl understandingly, "You just about made it, Sam."

"Just about," Sam agreed, and then said dutifully, "Jim, your missus wants you."

Jim Hoskins swore lazily and rose and said, "Bet this for me, Sam," and after that Marky Wolf made the introductions. Frank Beecham, the man Sam had already paired with the woman, was a gambler by profession, as his dress proclaimed. He had eyed Sam with suspicion since he entered the room, and now made no offer to shake hands.

He was a lean man, with a dissipated pale wedge

of a face, and his black eyes had a gall in them that stirred a slow anger in Sam. Without having to be told, he knew that the girl in the kitchen would never choose this man for a husband, so it was the remaining player whom Sam studied carefully after shaking his hand.

Carter McCune was the kind that made Sam Johns instinctively wary. He was a blond young man dressed in a rich black suit, but behind his tense smile and impatient good manners was a kind of arrogance that nothing could hide. It was in his hazel eyes, which were overlaid with a look of driving shrewdness that Sam had seen in the eyes of crooked horse-traders.

Sam sagged into a chair and beat his mind to alertness, for Jim Hoskins, like many a stage station owner, counted poker a more remunerative business than feeding and bedding travelers when the stage had to lay over. A greenhorn didn't stand a chance.

Sam hung on through two hands, his stomach aching with a miserable hunger, and then Mrs. Hoskins called him and he rose, watching for the game to break up.

But before he had left the room, it was settled that the game would go on three-handed, and Sam went out with the knowledge that Mrs. Hoskins was defeated, and not caring much.

There was only the girl in the kitchen, standing by the stove, and she nodded to the table where a place was set.

"Mrs. Hoskins said to eat."

Sam did. When he had wolfed down a plateful of steak and potatoes, the girl was there to help him to a second and they did not talk. Beyond, in one of the rooms, came the sound of a bitter argument being carried on in subdued voices between Jim and Mrs. Hoskins. The wind lashed the log walls and wailed above the creaking chimney. When Sam at last leaned back in his chair and reached for his sack of tobacco in his shirt pocket, he glanced up at the girl. She was half facing the range, her hands spread low over the lids, and her face was sad. The lamp in the wall bracket by the stove seemed to make a halo of light over her wheat colored hair.

Suddenly, she said without turning around, "Thanks for trying, anyway, Sam." She turned her head to look at him. "Has he lost much?"

Sam's face went hot, and he tried to look surprised.

"I overheard Mrs. Hoskins tell you," she said. "Has he lost much?"

Sam remembered the diminishing pile of gold coins in front of McCune and said, "Yes, ma'am," and concentrated on the cigarette he was making.

The girl didn't say anything for a long moment, and then she murmured in a low, bitter voice, "Have you ever watched everything you own trickle away into nothing, and know you couldn't stop it?"

"Yes, ma'am," Sam said quietly.

Slowly, the girl turned, surprise and doubt washing over her face.

"When?"

"Today."

She was silent a moment. "How was that?"

"Every head of cattle I own has been up in summer range in these mountains. Last week I come to round 'em up and drive them down." He looked down at his cigarette. "I didn't make it," he added briefly.

The girl looked searchingly at him and then turned back to the stove. Sam sat there in silence, feeling the strength and a kind of peace flow back into him, listening to the howling of the hurricane wind outside. The girl came over and sat in the chair opposite him, and when Sam glanced up she was looking into his eyes.

"Go on with it," she said.

"That's all there is."

"I don't mean that. It seems like we're in the same boat." Her voice dropped. "I saved that five hundred dollars teaching school. Carter was going to buy a share in Mr. Markham's store in Globe. We were going to be married. I want to hear what you're going to do now that you've lost your cattle."

Sam thought a minute.

"I don't know," he said at last. "I'm a pretty good cattleman. I couldn't call a fall blizzard, but I reckon I came as close to it as other cattlemen. I think the bank will loan me money. I'll try again."

"I can't try again!" the girl said passionately. "I began teaching school when I was sixteen, and I'm twenty-four now!"

Sam asked curiously, "Couldn't you stop him?"

"No."

Sam said something he knew was mealy-mouthed, then. "Maybe marriage will change him."

He was glad Mrs. Hoskins came into the kitchen then, because the girl would have said something she would have regretted. Sam rose and put his cigarette in the stove and then went into the front room, a dull anger riding him.

Sam had just put his back to the stove when Frank Beecham, the gambler, slammed his cards down and turned to the woman, fury in his voice. "My God, Trix, can't you make him shut up that coughing?"

Trix's hand ceased moving, and the coughing went on, a little more softly and just as insistent.

"The poor man's sick," Trix murmured, a touch of resentment in her voice and none in her eyes.

Beecham got up and stamped around the other players. Marky regarded him speculatively, as if wondering at his sudden nerves, and then looked at Trix. McCune tapped nervously on the back of his cards and said, "You've got a stake in that pot, Beecham."

"Hell with it!" Beecham snarled and came to rest beside Sam, his back to the stove. The little man was coughing again when the game was resumed.

Beecham glanced obliquely at Sam and said, "Which way'd you come?"

"East," Sam answered, distaste in his voice.

"From Van Horn?"

Sam was too weary to explain, and didn't want to anyway, so he told a half truth and said, "Yes," although it had been a week and a half since he had seen the town. He looked at the back of McCune's head and beat his tired brain toward thinking of a way to break up the game. Beecham, after a moment, said without turning around, "Come in here, Trix," and walked into one of the bedrooms. The woman followed him, and there was the look in her eyes of a dog who answers his master's call, not knowing whether he will be petted or cuffed. The little man coughed and coughed, his hand over his mouth.

Sam went over to the bench and sat beside him. He said gently, to him, "You're too close to the stove, partner. That heat makes you cough."

The little man sat up then, and smiled and said huskily, "Maybe you're right." He rose and moved across the room to a bench by the big table, and Sam leaned back against the, wall, watching McCune. He wasn't pretty to look at now, with his handsome face a little gray with excitement. With the ruthlessness acquired in a hundred saloons on a thousand nights, Jim Hoskins and Marky were taking turns at winning his money. Her money, Sam thought.

He was glad when at last McCune stood up and said, "Well, I'm cleaned, gentlemen."

Marky nodded and said with mild bluntness, "You don't know a hell of a lot about poker, Mister."

McCune laughed bitterly and tramped out into the kitchen. A sudden disgust welled up in Sam, disgust with McCune for losing the money and disgust with Marky for taking it. He went over to the table and sat down beside the little man, and because he did not want to think of what was going on right now between the girl and McCune in the kitchen, he felt a wild urge to talk, to blot it from his mind.

The little man looked at him shyly across the table, and when he got Sam's answering smile he reached in his vest and pulled out a wallet from which he took a card, and laid it in front of Sam. It was the business card of Kentucky Friends Distillery in Fort Worth. In a lower corner was printed 'Mr. Wiley Brokaw, Representative.'

"Ever drink our product?" the little man asked.

Sam grinned. "I might have."

"A sound sour-mash whiskey," the little man went on. He smiled shyly. "Never drink it myself. Can't. But I've sold it for years." He went on talking of the difference in whiskies, stopping to cough softly now and then, and Sam wondered what bitter necessity had driven him to a job for which he was so ill suited. And while Sam listened, the girl and McCune came back into the room. There had been bitter words out there in the kitchen, he could tell. McCune went to the stove and stood there sulking, while the girl came over and sat down beside the whiskey drummer and listened absently.

They were all this way, with Marky, lighted lantern at his feet, putting on his coat to have a look at the horses in the barn, and Beecham and Trixie still in the back room, when the sudden kick came on the front door. Then the latch bar lifted and a plume of riding snow hissed against the stove and a man stepped inside and leaned against the door to shut it.

He wore a faded blue army overcoat which somehow he had contrived to unbutton and open between the time he shut the door and when he turned to face the room; and Sam understood that necessity when Marky swung his lantern up to get a look at the man's face. It was the small face of a slight man, finely shaped and leaned down until every muscle showed, and above the full black mustache frozen stiffly, the color had been driven high into the cheekbones by the cold. Above them was a pair of alert, steady brown eyes.

If a man was in doubt about the face, he had only to look at the hands. For this stranger, now, was taking two mittens off his right hand, his gun hand, while his left hand was bare and white with the cold.

But Sam had no need to look at the hands. Once every two weeks for a year he had seen that face—on the yellowing reward poster nailed up beside the window at the postoffice. He even remembered that the printer had inserted a comma instead of a period in the big bold-faced line of type: "$5000,000 Reward, Dead or Alive."

Jim and his wife and Beecham and Trixie had all come into the room at the sound of the opening door; and now Sam watched these people, just as Lex Quayle, the outlaw, was watching them, and he saw what Lex saw; that three people—himself, Marky Wolf, and Carter McCune—knew the stranger; the rest were only curious.

Sam said gently, "Mrs. Hoskins, he's likely hungrier than I was."

"I can believe that on this night," Mrs. Hoskins said, and went into the kitchen.

"Let me help you off with that coat," Trixie said in a friendly, motherly way, and crossed over to him.

Beecham said sharply, "He's no cripple, Trix."

Marky Wolf said mildly, "I better look at them horses."

And Lex Quayle said in a regretful voice, "This storm cost me a mighty nice horse."

And the wind wailed and tore at the log building, while Carter McCune watched the outlaw with a kind of careful, taut interest. And Sam, knowing greed when he saw it in a man's eyes, knew that the seed, which had fallen on the barren soil of his own recognition, had taken hold in McCune. That sorry gambler of a man was already thinking that while he had dropped five hundred dollars tonight, five thousand dollars had just walked into the room and was his for the taking.

Lex Quayle saw it in McCune's face, too. His quick brown eyes took in McCune's figure, noting the absence of a gun belt, sizing him up as a potential threat, and then they dismissed him. He said to Trix with a brief smile, "I'll keep my coat on, thanks. I'm cold."

The friendliness in the whiskey-drummer's eyes glowed behind the fever as he looked at Quayle. "So you had to shoot your horse."

Quayle nodded faintly.

"That makes a man feel bad," the little man said, in sympathy.

"It does that," Quayle said, and there was something in his tone that said he was grateful.

Mrs. Hoskins came in and said, "You can eat now."

Quayle, with a sharp warning look at McCune, put his back to him and walked out into the kitchen. Mrs. Hoskins looked over the crowd and then announced, "Miss Virginia and me are going to sleep in the west room. The rest of you will have to make out the best you can with the bed and the cot in the other room."

She was looking at Trixie, and there was an implacable righteousness in her face, the look of a good woman who can safely be cruel to a bad one.

The little whiskey drummer said sturdily, "I guess we can fix the cot up for the other lady."

Mrs. Hoskins sniffed audibly. "If I was as sick as you are, I'd claim that cot and get some sleep."

She was still looking at Trix, whose face was getting hard with humiliation.

"I don't sleep much," the whiskey drummer said mildly. "She can have my bed and welcome."

Mrs. Hoskins went out, but Sam didn't notice her. He was watching McCune with a kind of dread gathering within him. McCune came over to the girl, and without any attempt at privacy he said in a low excited voice, "Virginia, do you know—"

Sam came to his feet, smacking his palm on the table. "Shut up!"

The cold fury of his voice cut through McCune's speech and brought silence.

"Sometimes," Sam said thickly, "mindin' your business means the difference between walkin' out of a place and bein' carried out. This is one of those times, McCune."

All of them were watching Sam, mystified, and now they looked at McCune. He regarded Sam a long time with those shrewd and cunning eyes and then he said sulkily, "All right," and went over to the stove and stoked it.

Sam knew the girl, Virginia, was watching him in a vain attempt to get a clue to his meaning.

He said dully, "I'm going to bed."

Beecham, off in the corner, said, "You ought to," but when Sam shuttled his hot gaze to stare at him, Beecham added hastily, "We all ought to."

Beecham followed Sam into the tiny room, and when Sam had lighted the lamp he looked around him. There was an iron double bed, piled high with blankets, and a cot. Beecham walked over to the cot and pulled off a boot.

"Get up," Sam said shortly.

Beecham looked up, mock innocence on his face. "You and McCune have got the bed. What are you kickin' about?"

"That cot is for Trix," Sam said gently, ominously.

"She's my woman. Let her sleep on the floor," Beecham sneered. "It won't be the first time."

Sam took a step toward him, and put both hands on his hips.

"Beecham," he said softly, "I've been wanting to make your face over ever since I saw it. I think I will."

Beecham caught the tone of his voice. In silence, he picked up his boot and moved over to the bed, his eyes sultry. Sam ripped a blanket from the bed, threw it on the cot, and carried both into the front room. He said good night, not looking at Virginia, and tramped back into the corridor. Quayle, still in his army coat, was standing at the kitchen end of the corridor. He said, "You. Come here."

He backed into the kitchen and Sam came up to face him. Quayle studied him a scant moment, then said, "You know me." It wasn't a question; it was a statement of fact."

"Yes."

"So does that counter-jumper in there."

"Yes."

Quayle stared levelly at him and said, "You don't look like a bounty hunter."

"I'm not."

Quayle almost smiled. He nodded his head toward the door. "That driver says there's blankets from the stage. Him and me will sleep in the loft." He paused, then added mildly, "I'm pretty easy to get along with if nobody crowds me."

"That's what I figured," Sam said.

"Just as long as both of you don't forget it,"

Quayle said amiably. "Good night." He wrapped his coat around him, and went out into the howling blackness.

It was still dark when Sam was roused by the sound of Jim Hoskins shaking the ashes from the big range in the kitchen. Sam rose and went into the big room to build a fire. The lamp was turned low on the table, and on a bench against the wall Mr. Wiley Brokaw, covered with Trix's buffalo coat, was asleep, his head on Trix's lap. She was sitting up, the blanket around her shoulders, and when she saw Sam she smiled sleepily.

"He got to sleep about an hour ago," she said quietly, looking over at the bench. "Poor man."

"He needs a rest," Sam said gently.

Trixie laughed without humor. "When you're supportin' your dead brother's kids on the money he gets, you don't take time to rest," she said grimly. "We talked last night, after you was all asleep." She looked at Sam. "He's all right, he is," she said quietly, and then added, with a trace of hopeless bitterness in her voice, "except he's goin' to kill hisself if he don't get some rest and women's food in him."

Sam built the fire quietly, thinking of the little whiskey drummer, and then of McCune, asleep in there with Beecham. One would wake to a lonely day of fighting against sickness; the other to the love of a woman far too good for him.

It angered Sam and he went out into the kitchen. When he was washed, he and Jim, bundled in all the clothes they could find, went out into the cold dawn to thaw out the pump and to water the stock. The dawn came still and cold and brittle as glass, with the sky the color of frost-rimmed steel. Sam was glad for work to do, for he did not like the idea of watching Virginia, knowing he was unable to help her. The sun had just laid a jagged saw-tooth of shadow over the spotless meadow as it came up through the far timber when the triangle clanged for breakfast. Jim, Marky and Sam tramped into the house, which was warm and smelling of bacon and coffee and the hot metal of the stove.

Virginia was helping Mrs. Hoskins carry the food into the big room up front, where the breakfast table was set. Sam did not look at her, did not want to. He went into the bedroom, peeled off his borrowed overcoat and mackinaw and hung them up. It was then he saw his gun-belt hanging on the nail where he had put it the night before.

His gun was gone.

He was standing there staring at the empty holster when he heard Virginia's voice say, "Good morning, Sam."

She was standing in the doorway, her hand holding the curtain back, a faint friendly smile on her face, and Sam thought she was the loveliest and saddest looking woman he had ever seen.

"I'm going to take my licking, just like you are," she said. "I just wanted you to know I wasn't going to quit."

"It'll be all right," Sam said. There was nothing else to say.

She went back into the kitchen, and Sam, troubled, went into the big room. They were all taking their places now, except Lex Quayle. He was standing by the stove, and his nod to Sam was amiable enough. Lex waited until Carter McCune chose a seat with his back to the room, and then Lex walked over and took the place beside him.

McCune said surlily, "I was saving that for Virginia."

Virginia, who was filling the cups from a huge pot of coffee, said quickly, "I'll help Mrs. Hoskins, Carter, and get a bite in the kitchen."

Sam saw Lex grin secretly into his plate at that, and then the swell of talk rose. Marky announced that he would take the empty stage after breakfast and break a trail across the deep snow of the meadow. If he succeeded in reaching the timber, he would come back for his passengers, certain that he would be able to make it from there on. Sam listened to all the talk in silence, and behind his silence was the memory of the stolen gun. Who had it? He thought he knew, and he hated himself for guessing the reason. Marky soon rose and went out, and Jim Hoskins followed, while Beecham finished and sat back picking his teeth, glaring at Trix and the little whiskey drummer, who sat together at the far end of the table.

It was while Virginia was leaning across to fill Sam's cup that Lex Quayle raised a hand and said sharply, "Quiet, everybody!"

The talk died off. They all looked at Quayle, who had his head cocked to one side, as if listening.

A faint halloo, far off in the winter morning, came to them, and Mrs. Hoskins, in the doorway, said, "It's the upstage at the edge of the meadow, I'll declare. They'll probably want Jim to help them break a trail across."

Lex Quayle, his face taut, rose and hurried to the window.

And then, because Lex's back was turned, it happened.

Carter McCune rose steathily, stepped over the

bench, and even as he moved his right hand went
to his hip pocket. He was just swinging up Sam's
gun when Sam, at last fighting free of the bench,
dived across the table. He slammed into McCune's
back, and on the heel of it came the shot, and then
they went down together.

There was a faint jangle of glass after the shot
and Lex whipped around, a gun already in his hand,
to see Sam drive McCune to the floor.

McCune's gun skidded across the floor, and he
rolled to his knees. Sam came up to face him, and
without looking at Lex he said, "Don't do it,
Lex!"

McCune's face was livid with rage, and in his
anger he had even forgotten that Lex could shoot
him. He came at Sam, arms flailing, and Sam
drove a blow against his jaw that slammed him
back against the wall, shaking the timbers.

Sam said through his teeth, "Damn your yellow
belly, you go careful!"

"Carter!" Virginia cried.

But McCune was lost to advice. He came in
again, great sobs of anger choking him. And then
Sam did what he had been wanting to do for so
long. He lost his temper. With a low growl, he
swept McCune's guard aside and drove a fist into
his midriff, and then laced over a hook that sent
McCune back against the wall again. But this time
Sam did not wait for him to come away. Feet
planted wide, he moved in, his heavy fists slogging
in wide arcs and beating a sickening rhythm on
McCune's body and face.

The hurt of it sobered McCune and he tried to
cover up, but all the hate and contempt that had
been riding Sam these long hours had come to a
head. He fought with a savage, merciless brutality,

and even McCune's kicks could not stop him. He grabbed McCune's hair and yanked back his head, and then with his free hand he beat his face time and again, and when his hold slipped, McCune sagged to the floor like an empty sack and lay there at his feet.

Sam stirred his body with the toe of his boot, the last gesture of contempt, and then turned away from him, and found himself facing Lex Quayle.

"You made a mistake," Quayle said shortly. "You should have let me have him." He raised a hand to his hat brim in a kind of sardonic salute. "I'm proud to have met a man whose idea of a fair target is not my back. Thanks." He nodded to the rest of them and then headed for the kitchen. Passing the table, he flipped a gold piece onto it, and then they heard him closing the back door.

Marky Wolf, who had come in during the fight, announced in that silence, "Better get your wraps, folks. We'll try to break our half the trail loaded."

The rest of them moved toward their coats—all except Virginia. She stood beside Sam, looking down at McCune, and Sam did not know what to say.

It was she who spoke first.

"Can you get him into his coat?" she asked.

While she was getting the coat, Sam hoisted McCune's sagging body to the bench. His nose was bleeding all over his clothes, and one eye was swelling shut and his mouth was cut, and he kept shaking his head from side to side. Marky Wolf, burly in his great buffalo coat, stood in the middle of the floor, grinning at the sight of him.

There was a sudden raising of voices in the bedroom, and then the sound of flesh smacking flesh. Beecham's voice said angrily, "Trix! Come back here!"

Trix came out of the corridor running, and headed for the front door. She tugged vainly at the big bolt as Beecham elbowed past Mrs. Hoskins and strode after her.

Marky raised a burly arm and barred his way.

"What's the matter?" Marky drawled.

Beecham's face was ugly with anger. He raised a thin arm and pointed to Trix. "That damn wench robbed me!"

"You're a liar!" Trix said hotly.

Mrs. Hoskins said, "I'll have none of that talk!" in a stern voice.

But Trix had been pushed too far. She said to Marky, "Frank won seven thousand dollars in a crooked poker game at Van Horn two days ago. He's runnin' away now." She pointed to Sam. "Frank thought this man had been sent after him last night to get the money, so he gave it to me to keep."

She looked at Frank and sneered. "I gave it back to him—all but five hundred dollars. And I put that in Mr. Brokaw's wallet last night when he slept. He needs it worse than that tin-horn!"

Marky's hand came down, as Beecham yelled, "You're lying."

Marky said, "Wait a minute." To Mrs. Hoskins he said, "Will you have a free bed for a couple of days, Mrs. Hoskins?"

Puzzled, and still outraged, Mrs. Hoskins said, "Why—yes."

"Good," Marky said. He took off his mitten and hit Frank Beecham in the face as hard as he could swing. Beecham fell as if struck by lightning.

Marky, rubbing his knuckles, said, "All right, put him in it, Mrs. Hoskins."

They headed for the door and Virginia, came into the room with McCune's.

In silence, Sam held McCune erect while Virginia put his coat and hat on. Afterwards, between them they carried him out to the stage.

Trix and Brokaw, side by side, sat in the seat facing the horses, robes pulled up to their chins. McCune, at sight of the stage, stopped and wrenched free of Sam's grip. He turned to Virginia and muttered hotly, "I did it for money, Virginia! If he hadn't stopped me, we would have had five thousand dollars!"

"Get in," Virginia said patiently.

McCune straightened up and took Virginia's elbow.

"After you," he said coldly.

Virginia freed her elbow.

"I'm not going, Carter," she said quietly. "I could live with a fool, maybe. But I could not live with a man who would shoot another man in the back for money." She stepped away. "Good-by, and good luck. I'll never see you again."

"But—"

Marky Wolf put a hand on his arm. "You heard her. Get in."

McCune gave Virginia one last bitter, helpless glance, and then he climbed in. Marky swung up in the seat, picked up the ribbons, and Jim Hoskins let go the lead horse's bit. The teams plunged into the deep snow. Behind the stage was Lex Quayle, mounted on one of Hoskins' horses. He nodded gravely as he passed Sam and Virginia, standing together in the deep snow of the yard.

Both of them watched while the two stages, their teams laboring in great clouds of steam rising from their backs, slogged through the snow until they met in the middle of the meadow. They saw Lex Quayle put his horse out into the snow and pull past the two stages to the broken trail beyond, and then put spurs to his horse and vanish into the timber.

Virginia sighed then, and looked up at Sam. "Thanks, Sam—for everything."

"You're going back?"

"To teach school again," Virginia said quietly.

Sam put both hands on her arms and turned her around to face him.

"Not while I can talk," he said. He started to say something, and it wouldn't come. Three times he tried, and failed.

Finally, he said, "I've got something to ask you, Virginia. Maybe I can ask it before we get to Van Horn."

Virginia smiled softly and said, "I will listen to you this time too, Sam."

Exile

The first snow of the year 1863 was rolling off the Navajo country to the west, driving slantwise into the shallow bowl of barren hills that held Fort Defiance. It was a snow such as only the Navajo country gets, wet and heavy and riding on a persistent wind.

It had a quality so completely personal and vindictive that the sentry at the east gate of the fort was moved to say sourly to his companion, "This'll tie up them sutlers' wagons in adobe mud till they won't get chopped out by next spring."

He was leaning against the door of the rough sentry box for protection, a scarf tied around his ears. Already, the space in front of the gate was a pool of slush soon to be trampled into mud.

Behind him, the few low buildings of the fort were lighted against the midafternoon dusk. The sentry's companion only grunted and hunkered down in the sentry box, determined to make the most of his turn at the shelter.

The sentry box faced east, so that they both saw the figure of the rider and his pack horse at the same time. Neither spoke about it, but rather watched the man beat his way to them against the tide of the wind and the snow.

When he approached, they both fell out and barred his way and regarded him as he pulled his horse into the shelter of the sentry box. He was a tall figure, muffled in the thick blue coat of the Union Army issue, but there the military clue was lost. His saddle was a western rig caked with the soft snow and his broad-brimmed hat was a Stetson, not the cavalry black.

"Hell of a day, boys," he observed in a drawling voice. His laugh was slow, short. "This is a tough depot to find."

"There's a road under the snow if you can see it," the grinning sentry replied. "Where you from?"

"East."

"The war?"

"Some time back, yes."

The sentry walked closer to get a look at his man, who was half turned and tugging at the lead rope of his surly looking pack horse. Afoot, he would be over six feet, the sentry judged, and he had a thin, weather-burnished face that held the good-humored carelessness of a born western man. Moreover, he cursed his horse with a tolerant abusiveness no easterner could have commanded.

The sentry, satisfied, said mournfully, "Wisht we'd see some of that war."

"You're lucky you don't," Tom Curtin replied gently. "Besides, I understand you've got one here."

"Only agin' them Navyhos," the sentry said, grinning. "It ain't a war and it ain't a fight, hardly." He stepped back and said, "Pass on, sir."

Tom Curtin touched the brim of his hat and pushed his horse past the sentries. Beyond, the snow blanketed the rough parade ground flanked by small mounds of debris as yet uncleared after the summer's disastrous fire. At the far end of the grounds, he could see where the new buildings were going up. Orderly rows of tents were stretched out on the south side.

But it was over toward the north and under the cliff that Tom Curtin's gaze finally settled. The snow was not so thick that he could not make out the sorry cluster of canvas tents and brush shelters and makeshift Navajo hogans that lay over that way, and he pulled his horse over to look.

Paused near them, he reined up and observed this camp, his face grave and troubled. He had seen the same thing over back at Fort Wingate, where hundreds upon hundreds of Navajo refugees, starved, beaten, without goods or property, stripped of hope, utterly dependent on the white man's whim, were waiting to go into exile. It was not a pretty sight and he turned away from it now, trying not to look at the silent expectant children and older men who had come out of their crude shelters to observe him. He would come back to them later.

Everywhere around the fort, it seemed, building had been stopped by the snow. There was arising out of the litter of boards and stone some plan of construction which had a military order, but mostly it was turmoil. Work had ceased during the storm and stubbornly the snow was smoothing over the harsh corners of the construction. One row of single-story buildings with an awninged porch running across the front was finished, and it was for this that Tom Curtin headed. A flag, whipping soddenly in the storm, proclaimed that it was headquarters.

He dismounted at the building, leading his horses around to the lee side out of wind, and then mounted the porch. A sentry at the door came to attention, and Tom Curtin asked to see the commanding officer, Major Hinstead. He was admitted to a small anteroom holding a desk in one corner. Deal benches lined the wall and overhead a kerosene lamp burned brightly against the gray day outside.

An adjutant in blue took his name and then disappeared through a door in the back partition. Soon, he came out to usher Curtin into the office beyond.

Behind a littered desk in the middle of the room sat a heavy-built, kindly looking man in army blue, his tunic unbuttoned. The room was thick with cigar smoke, warm and comfortable after the weather outside.

Tom Curtin saluted smartly and at a nod from Major Hinstead stepped forward and extended a paper.

The major opened it and glanced at it and then rose and extended his hand. "Pleasure to meet you, Lieutenant Curtin. Sit down." He gestured to a chair and extended a box of cigars to Tom, who took one.

Under this pale light, he was a contrast to the major. His clothes were unmilitary, a pair of worn army trousers tucked into half-boots, a gray checked flannel shirt and black neckerchief showing under the army greatcoat which he now took off and laid on a bench. He was a tall man with a lithe, lazy way of moving. His cheeks seemed a little gaunted, his face fatigued, but his gray eyes were keen and almost tranquil as he sized up the room. On a side wall was a large map extensively blue-penciled and showing the battle lines of the Union Armies. A framed picture of Lincoln hung nearby. An American flag, a framed picture of the major's class at West Point and an Apache bow and arrow quiver hung on the opposite wall.

Tom accepted the major's light and they both sat down. Major Hinstead leaned back in his chair and regarded his visitor amiably.

"Not much chance of getting war news from you, Lieutenant, I take it," he said.

"Hospital news only," Tom said, laughing.

The major gestured to the paper. "I notice you've got a six months' leave. Doesn't sound optimistic for the end of the war, does it?"

"That was a gift," Tom said. "I was pretty well stove up when they exchanged me."

"From a Confederate prison?"

Tom nodded. "You'll notice that's sick leave."

Major Hinstead grinned. "So I noticed. You look all right to me and still you've three months more leave."

"It was a special favor," Tom replied. He puffed slowly on his cigar and then said suddenly, "You see, Major, I've got a little job out in this country."

"Official?"

Tom shook his head and leaned forward in his seat. "It depends almost entirely on your generosity, Major."

"How so?"

"I want to join up with your New Mexico volunteers for this Navajo campaign."

Slowly, Major Hinstead puffed on his cigar, his eyes probing. He said finally, "That's queer. I mean, if you want to fight, the Union Army could find more use for you in the south than I could here.''

"Let me explain," Tom said. "You see, I'm not green in this Indian fighting. I was born in a fort down in the Apache country."

"So?" Major Hinstead said politely. Tom could sense the curiosity collecting behind the major's polite exterior.

"That's where the story begins," Tom went on. "I spent all my boyhood at Fort Taylor in the Apache country."

"Most of my volunteers have fought Indians of some sort."

Tom leaned back. This was going to be hard to explain, especially to a man who could not help but have the views of Major Hinstead. Tom wracked his brain for a new approach and decided to chance it.

"It was back in St. Louis that I heard about General Carleton's decision to clean up the Navajos," he began. "You see, it was rather a personal matter to me."

Hinstead said nothing.

"When I was a kid," Tom went on, "my dad bought a small Navajo boy from the Apaches, who were holding him as a slave. He was just my age. That was back in '52." Tom paused. "He was the best friend I ever had, that Navajo boy."

The major's eyebrows lifted a little.

"When I heard about this campaign against the Navajos, I had my leave. I decided to come out and find out about Johnny Dinah, my Navajo friend."

"Dinah? That's a queer name."

"The Navajos call themselves The Dineh or The People," Tom said. "Little Johnny's name was twisted to Dinah by the soldiers."

"What about him?"

"When I left the war, he went back to his people."

Major Hinstead put down his cigar. "How well do you know the history of this campaign, Lieutenant?" he asked slowly. "I suppose you know that the Navajos have broken seven separate treaties with us. That they've butchered your own people as well as the Mexicans. You must know what they are—a thieving, murdering lot that have got to be wiped out. General Carleton gave them all warning. On last July twentieth, Colonel Kit Carson set out from here to conquer them. He put out word among them that if they didn't want war, they could come here to Defiance or Wingate and surrender." He shrugged. "If your Johnny Dinah is the man you think he is, he should be at Fort Wingate right now, one of the surrendered Navajos who want peace."

"But he isn't," Tom murmured.

"And he's not here," the major said. "Therefore, he must be one of those braves who want to fight us."

"I don't believe it."

"Facts speak for themselves," the major said bluntly. "When we started withdrawing soldiers from our western posts for the war with the south, the Navajos started raiding. They were warned and offered peace. All who accepted it were pardoned. All who didn't are going to be killed or captured."

"There must be exceptions," Tom said stubbornly.

"Perhaps."

Tom sat up straight. "At any rate, Major, that's the favor I want of you—permission to join Kit Carson's volunteers and to find Johnny Dinah and bring him back with me."

"He's very likely dead now."

"He wouldn't fight a white man."

The major opened his mouth to protest and then closed it again. He looked at Tom shrewdly and for a long while and then sighed. Straightening up, he rummaged through a sheaf of papers on his desk until he found the one he was looking for. He read it and then said, "This came in from Carson's regiment by courier today. It was sent five days ago. He says that in ten days he will be ready to raid the Navajos in their stronghold, the Canyon de Chelly." He looked up at Tom. "If you hurry, you'll very likely get in on that campaign."

"You mean I have your permission, Major?" Tom said quickly.

Major Hinstead rose. "You have. I think it's insane, however. I've never seen one of the murdering Navajo sons yet that was worth more than the powder to kill him. You'll find your friend fighting your country's troops, I'm certain, and the Lord knows what breach of authority I'm committing in letting you try to bring him back." His face softened a little bit. "You're doing this because of a childhood friendship, nothing else?" he asked.

Tom nodded.

"You don't look like a fool, Lieutenant Curtin," the major said gently, "but you sound suspiciously like one. However, you know your own mind. I think"—and here his voice became astringent, amused—"that you've earned the right to die in your own way. I'm at your service."

"Thank you, sir," Tom said.

"Just one word of warning," the major said, as Tom rose. "This isn't a very pretty fight. Our troops are volunteers, Mexicans mostly. They've got a hundred years' grudge against those murdering Navajos. Our scouts are Utes and Zunis and they've fought with Navajos since before the Spaniards arrived. You'll see things you won't like, but try and remember why."

"I've been to war, Major," Tom said.

"I'm trying to remember that," Major Hinstead said drily. "Good day, sir."

The snow stopped at midnight and Lieutenant Tom Curtin set out, armed with a new rifle of army issue, three blankets, a new .44 Colt's revolver which he wore rammed in his belt and a letter of introduction to Colonel Christopher Carson inside which was folded his commission as lieutenant in the New Mexico Volunteers.

His departure was quick and he was almost curt to the stable sergeant who helped him saddle and waved an amiable good-bye. For Tom Curtin had left the mess hall that evening and had gone straight to the temporary hogans of the surrendered Navajos, and what he had heard there disheartened him. His first two hours there, sitting on the sheepskins before two old men, were irritating. He was trying to conjure up out of his youth the almost forgotten Navajo language which Johnny Dinah had taught him. These he pieced out with Apache, which was understood by these men who were of the *Tshí-ji* clan and distant cousins of the Apaches. All his talk, of course, was directed toward finding Johnny Dinah, the son of Hosteen Tla of the *Loó hak di-neh' eh* clan. Could they tell him of him? At first they could not. They were people of the south, but there were people of the north here in camp. Get them, said Tom. At last, an old woman and her daughter, half-starved and miserable beyond words, were ushered into the hogan. They took their seats to the right of center, as is custom. Upon questioning, they remembered Johnny Dinah, or Chee, as his Navajo name 'was. They had left him at Canyon de Chelly, but that was not his home. Far to the north in the Chuska mountains was where he and his wife's people lived. They hated the white man, his wife's people did, and they had promised to fight. They were a rich family, *ricos*. Some of them were already on their way to the Grand Canyon with their sheep, but the others would fight.

Tom listened with heavy heart. To a man who did not understand Navajo customs, it would have seemed fairly simple to go find Johnny Dinah and persuade him to surrender. But to Tom, who understood that a Navajo husband submits to the dictates of his wife's clan, for better or worse, it was not encouraging. It meant that unless he found Johnny Dinah first, he would perish with the foolish people of his wife's clan.

Tom listened for three hours to the complaints of these people, and, like General Carleton and Captain Dodge and Kit Carson before him, he was saddened. Here was a people who had warred all through its history, who made it a point of pride to fight and raid and steal. They could not understand the white man's ways. Most of them were ready to abide by the white man's decision and cease their plundering, but the young hotheads of the Navajos would not hear of it. In their overweening pride they thought they could conquer the white man. And now, a whole nation of people was being punished for the sins of a few. Their sheep were being killed, their crops destroyed, and now, while the white man was hunting them to the very bases of their four sacred mountains, they were starving here. They could not eat the food the army gave them; they did not know how to prepare it. Where were they going? Were they going to be killed?

Tom left without giving them an answer, for he did not know it himself. He did not take leave of Major Hinstead, for the hour was late and besides, he did not want to face him. Hinstead's contempt, polite and obvious, had galled him all through the mess. If Hinstead did not already know that the color of a man's skin is no gage of his heart, then he could not be told.

Outside the fort, Tom headed north and west toward Canyon de Chelly. The sky had cleared and the country was a spotless blanket of white under the moon, with the stunted cedars and pinons, stippling it with black. Far off there to the north and west, waiting in Canyon de Chelly, was smiling Johnny Dinah, tall, gravely courteous, his face probably as impassive as the rock cliffs that hovered over him. He knew the white man and his terrible ways, but he would loyally stay with his wife's people. And soon, maybe, some Mexican sheepherder, conscripted from the rough guerilla wars of the border, would face Johnny with a gun. And Johnny would only have a bow and arrows to defend himself and his people. He would fight and die, this man who had been a gentle, lovable boy and who had loved Tom's mother and father until he had been willing to die for them in his gratitude.

It could not happen!

Daylight found Tom on a low tilting plateau. The thaw started as soon as high sunup and the snow, so smooth and unrelenting during the night, began to sag and melt. There was no trail to follow, for Kit Carson's volunteers had split up into small raiding bands.

Once, on the third day riding between high fawn-colored mesas in an empty vast country, Tom came across a trail of riders. The snow was patchy now and he could follow the trail. It took him into a box canyon and he followed it out. There he found a sight that sickened him. What had been a hogan was ashes. Buzzards rose at his approach and lazily wheeled off overhead; the stench was sickening. A herd of a hundred sheep had been killed in the brush corral against the base of the cliff. They lay piled in bloated heaps. Halfway to the hogan there was a small Navajo boy stretched out under a tree where the snow covering him had not yet melted. He had been shot and scalped, and it did not take Tom long to understand who had done it. The Zunis did not scalp and neither did the Mexicans. This was the handiwork of Kit Carson's Ute scouts whom he had brought down with him from the north and armed with rifles.

Once more the next day Tom found the same thing, only this time it was a Navajo herder and his grown son. That day Tom struck a trail heading in the direction he was going. In the night it snowed again.

And early on the morning of the fifth day he came upon the camp of the volunteers. The two companies were breaking camp as Tom rode in. He asked the way to the commanding officer's tent and picked his way through the mass of men knocking down tents and putting out the fires. The snow that had come in the night made the work arduous and the volunteer troops—mostly Spanish-Americans with a scattering of Americans—were bundled up against the sharp cold of this high plateau. Occasionally, in the crowd, he would see some of the Zuni scouts. They also, were armed.

The headquarters tent was in the middle of the camp and four or five men, three of them in army blue, were gathered there outside, directing camp breaking. A stove inside the tent pillared blue cedar smoke up into the clear cold sky.

Captain Albert Pfeiffer was the commanding officer and he received Tom pleasantly. A rough table stood in the middle of the brush-floored tent and packing boxes were the only seats. Pfeiffer was a tall, scholarly looking man and his glance at Tom's credentials was cursory. He looked up from them and said, "That's an unusual commission, Lieutenant Curtin. Of course it's all right with me. You are free to come and go—only I wouldn't advise leaving the camp alone."

"You expect a heavy fight, then?" Tom asked.

By way of answer, Pfeiffer rose and put on his hat and took Tom's arm. Outside, they threaded their way through the confusion till they were at the western outpost of the camp. Pfeiffer was asking questions about the war in the east and Tom was answering. Suddenly, Tom noticed a gap in the plateau directly ahead. Curious, he watched it more closely as they approached. The gap, he could see now, was a canyon, but as he went on he could see it getting deeper and deeper.

Finally, when they were on the rim, he looked down. The land had fallen away sheer. Far below, six hundred feet, he could see the floor of the canyon. The vastness of it caught at his breath. On a dark night, a stranger might ride unsuspecting into this and walk his horse off into sheer space. The canyon twisted away to the north and the west and was soon lost to sight between gargantuan walls.

"That's where the Indians are holed up," Pfeiffer said calmly. "Does it look like they'll put up a fight?"

When Tom nodded, the captain said, "Personally, I think it's almost suicide to try it. They say the whole Navajo nation is down there. But my volunteers are a tough lot. They want to clean up for good." He pointed off up the canyon and Tom could see a thin line of men going single file down the opposite side of the canyon. Below, in the canyon floor, men with shovels were working in the drifted snow, clearing a trail. "They won't even wait for a thaw," Pfeiffer added. "They're going to dig their way to them."

A bugle sounded behind them and they made their way back to camp. Already, the volunteers were leaving on their way to the canyon floor. Pfeiffer had told Tom that Colonel Carson, with the rest of the troops, had made a long circle west to plug up the mouth of the canyon. The strategy here was characteristic of Carson, who understood Indians and their way of fighting. He did not so much want to massacre the Navajos as to starve them out.

By plugging up both ends of the canyon, the Indians themselves could escape by climbing up the cliff side. But their horses, their many bands of sheep, their winter stores, the prized fruit trees and their homes would all be destroyed. It was swift and the most humane way to bring defeat.

On the canyon floor, several platoons of men were already digging a trail through the high drifts of snow and making it wide enough for horses and the mess wagons, which would follow.

The first skirmish occurred that afternoon two miles down the canyon. The tension among the men was high. The whole Navajo nation, the rumor went, was forted up here to fight to the death. But when they saw ahead of them only a small band of twelve Indians, timidly watching their progress toward them, they laughed. Was this the battle they were walking toward?

When the first platoon of volunteers was within rifle shot, a Zuni interpreter mounted a snowbank and called for the waiting Indians to surrender. His answer was a jeer and a volley of arrows which all fell short. Pfeiffer, more amused than angry, ordered a warning volley, and five seconds after it rang out in the still cold air, the Navajos turned and ran.

Minutes later, when the volunteers had made their way to where the Indians had been, they saw a low-roofed hogan against the cliff. It had been hidden by snowbanks.

"Carefully," a big Mexican cautioned. He gestured to the Zuni interpreter and the two of them, under the eyes of the other volunteers, cautiously approached the hogan. The Zuni was in the lead. He stooped down to enter the low door of the

hogan, rifle in hand, when suddenly he dodged out
and swung up his rifle.

"Come out!" he called in Navajo, then turned
and held up two fingers to the other volunteers.
"Come out and surrender!" he called again.

A man's voice from the inside of the hogan
answered, "O!"

At this, the big Mexican cursed and swung into
the doorway of the hogan. He raised his rifle
hip-high and shot. There was a tiny moan. Immediately following, there was a twang of a bow string
and the Mexican was slammed back out into the
snow. He dropped his rifle, put both hands to his
chest, then half turned and fell on his face. The
volunteers could see the arrow now. It was buried
in his chest almost to the feathers.

For one brief instant there was silence, and
then five of the Mexican volunteers exploded into
action.

But Tom Curtin was already moving. He made
the door first and turned to face the Mexicans, gun
in hand.

"Get back!" he ordered sharply, his voice cold
and savage. The Mexicans stopped, surprise in
their faces.

"But *señor*," one said. "You saw our friend
shot!"

"He was a fool," Tom said. "The Zuni told the
man inside to surrender and the man answered
'O', which is yes in Navajo. Your friend thought
he said no. Now get back and give the men a
chance."

For a few seconds, facing them, Tom did not
know what would happen. They were in an ugly

mood, with a dead friend at their feet, but he stood his ground, looking at each of them.

"But a Navajo, *senor!*" one protested angrily.

"He killed in self-defense!" Tom said angrily. "Now stand back. I will bring him out."

The Mexicans fell back a little. Tom turned and called in Navajo, "Drop your bows and come out. There are many of us."

Almost immediately a tall Navajo stepped out. He was clad in buckskin and was without weapons. His face was proud as he stepped out and surveyed his captors, and then his glance fell to the dead Mexican. A look of contempt filled his eyes, but his face did not change.

"Where is the other?" Tom asked in Navajo.

"Dead."

Tom went into the hogan. When his eyes became accustomed to the darkness, he saw an old woman sitting against the far wall, her head on her chest. One look at her told him the Mexican's ball had done its work well. He went out again and said to the Navajo, "The woman, who is she?"

"My mother," the Navajo answered quietly.

Tom turned to the waiting Mexicans. "Your friend was twice a fool. It was a woman he killed." He had the advantage now and he intended to keep it. "Colonel Carson will be proud of his soldiers," he said contemptuously. "What kind of men are you who make war on women?" He turned away and raised his voice so the others could hear him. "This man is my prisoner and he is not to be harmed." To the Mexicans he said, "Get about your business. Burn the hogan now and leave the woman in it."

He gestured to the Navajo who followed him. Soon, the work of destruction began. The hogan

with the old woman inside was burned. This was
the Navajo burial custom, Tom knew. All the
grain that could be found was heaped in the hogan
and burned also. The band of two hundred sheep
in the tiny canyon corral beyond was slaughtered,
serving as target practice for the laughing volunteers.
Meanwhile, a dozen axemen destroyed the large
orchard which crossed the canyon floor.

That night, they camped down canyon below
the burned hogan. Several huge fires were built
and the men relaxed around them. If this was a
sample of Indian fighting, they didn't mind it. The
horses and provisions had caught up with them
before dark.

Tom and his captive ate roast kid at one of the
big fires. When Pfeiffer and his officers had re-
tired to a temporary tent to plan the next day's
campaign, Tom beckoned the Navajo aside. They
squatted against a huge pile of bedrolls away from
the fire.

"What are you called?" Tom asked him in
Navajo.

"Hosteen Nez."

"Tall Man. All right, Tall Man. You are my
prisoner and my slave."

"Yes."

Tom smoked in silence for a moment. "Are
there many of your people in the canyon?"

"Few. They will not come back now. They
cannot fight against the firesticks. Against bows
and arrows, yes. Against the firestick, no."

Tom did not speak for a while. "The son of
Hosteen Tla, Chee—is he in the canyon?"

The Navajo did not answer and Tom spoke
sharply, "Answer, Tall Man."

"You will kill him."

"Did I kill you?"

"No. You saved my life. Will you save Chee's life?"

"Have you never heard of the white friend of Chee, the man he lived with in the south country?"

The Navajo started. "Many times. When Asson Tsosie's clan come to get the peaches in the fall, Chee tells us. Are you the white friend?"

"I am."

"Then it is an honor to be captured by such a warrior."

Tom made an impatient gesture. "Where is Chee?"

"He is north, at his wife's home in the Chuska mountains. His wife, Asson Tsosie, the Slim One, is of a powerful clan and they will fight."

"But they cannot."

"I know that. Chee knows that. But the others, they do not. They will fight the white man."

"These Chuska mountains, you know them?"

"I was there once."

"Can you take me to them?"

The Navajo hesitated. "They will kill you," he said. "Even Chee cannot stop them."

"But you, Tall Man, will you take me there?"

The Navajo shrugged. "I am your slave," he said tonelessly. "Whatever you wish."

Tom sat there, letting his pipe go out. Johnny Dinah was safe for a while, but only if Tom got to him before the clan arranged to fight. But the Chuska mountains were far distant. In his talk with the volunteers that day, Tom had quizzed them. They knew and the mountains, but only by sight. They were wild distant, inhabited by a fighting

clan whom the Mexicans were willing to let alone.
Only a few whites had ever been there.

Tom looked covertly at Hosteen Nez. He had
his guide now but it would be risky. A man on the
trail cannot go forever without sleep, and once he
was sleeping, what would prevent Hosteen Nez
from killing him? It was the warrior's game. The
only thing that would save him from Hosteen Nez,
Tom knew, was his friendship for Johnny Dinah.
These people, like all primitive folk, honored
friendship. Suddenly, the solution occurred to him.

He drew his revolver and extended it to Hosteen
Nez, who took it, looking at him. "You are not
my slave, Tall Man. You are my friend. Chee's
friends are my friends. I give you the firestick to
show you are equal with me. And tomorrow we
will go find Chee and save him from the foolish-
ness of his wife's people. Is it well?"

"It is well," Hosteen Nez said solemnly.

Late that night Tom made his claim to Captain
Pfeiffer and told him his plan. "You won't be
alive another day," Pfeiffer said shortly, when he
had heard.

"Still, I'd like two horses," Tom said stubbornly.

Pfeiffer shrugged. "Help yourself, then."

Before sunup the next morning, Tom and Hosteen
Nez set out back of the canyon. At sunrise they
climbed up to the plateau and headed north over
the long plateau and within two hours Tom knew
that Hosteen Nez had kept his word. He was his
friend.

On the second day they were riding through a long
rolling forest of scrub cedar. It was a strange
country, like nothing Tom had ever seen before.
Off through the trees to the west he could look out

over great white plains cut with vast mesas. These were a riot of color, red and purple and fawn and green, like fists thrust up from some great subterranean color pot. The distances he could see were so vast that they were staggering and the clear winter air seemed to magnify them. This was a country, he felt, that was never described by the white man, and never, in a hundred years of exploring it, would it ever be fully known.

They met several Navajos and to each of them Hosteen Nez announced that the white man was his prisoner. It was the safest way. But to all invitations to stop at hogans he turned a deaf ear. Once, he picked up a rumor that the Utes were raiding to the north and that they had firesticks now. The Navajos were all concerned. Could it be that the Utes would now conquer The People? And was it true that the white man to the east was warring on them? Strange stories had come up from Canyon de Chelly. Hosteen Nez did not have the heart to tell them the truth, that within a few weeks' time the white man would be hunting them. He said only that it was unwise to fight the white man, for he was the best of warriors.

On the third day they approached the Chuska mountains. They rose sheer out of a plain of greasewood, and for the first hundred feet of their rise they were of a soft orange rock that was so bright it hurt the eyes. Farther up, the rock gave way to tall timber. It was on the banks of Red Creek, Hosteen Nez had learned, that Asson Tsosie's clan lived. They started the climb up the creek bottom, but soon had to leave it for a trail. Just at dark, on the edge of the deep pine forest, they came to a clearing. Five winter hogans were raised

in the center and off toward the creek was the huge
sheep and horse corral.

A man stood in the clearing and at sight of them
he turned and called to the others. Indians seemed
to pour out of the hogans and they approached
cautiously. And then, running from one hogan, came
a tall, lithe Navajo man in buckskin.

"Johnny!" Tom shouted, dismounting.

The Navajo stopped and for one brief second he
was immobile, and then he said cautiously, "Tom?"

"It's me, Johnny!"

Johnny Dinah ran then. He and Tom shook
hands, and Johnny stroked the sleeve of his coat,
his face wreathed in smiles. He was almost Tom's
height, straight as one of the native pines, with a
thin nose, deepset eyes and a smile that was as warm
as friendship could make it. It warmed Tom's
heart to see him.

"How did you get here?" Johnny asked in halt-
ing English. "Your mother, how is she?"

Johnny had his mouth open to ask a thousand
more questions when a heavy, surly-looking Indian seized him by the arm and whirled him around.
The other men collected now in a tight circle
around them. Hosteen Nez watchfully stood guard
at Tom's right hand.

The surly man said in a swift spatter of Navajo,
"This is a white man, Chee. Do you not see?"

"I see," Johnny said gravely. "He is my friend."

"He is white!" another Indian said sharply.
"Kill him."

Johnny whirled to confront this man. "You will
die if you touch him!"

The swart Indian laughed and seized Tom's arm.
Like an explosion, Johnny was on top of him and

they fell to the ground. The Navajo does not fight
with his fists; he wrestles instead. And this was
Johnny's way of fighting for his friend. There was
a swift movement between the two on the ground,
a grunt, and then Johnny was on his knees. He had
the surly man's arm bent back in a hammer lock
behind his back. And holding him so, Johnny
staggered to his feet, holding the man like a baby
in his arms. He raised him head high with a mighty
heave, then threw him to the earth. The force of
the fall shook the ground. The man gagged for air,
half turned over, then rolled over on his back, his
eyes unseeing.

Johnny turned swiftly to confront the others.
''What now?''

''He is of our clan, Chee!'' one man said angrily.
It was the signal for them to swarm on Johnny.
They pinned his arms behind him and then turned
to Tom. Tom lashed out with a left that sent their
leader sprawling, and then too late, he thought of
his gun. He had it half out when they dived at
him. He sprawled back on the snow and then they
were all jumping on him. Something rapped his
head and he saw a pinwheel of stars in the dusk
sky before sight went black and bottomless.

When he came to, he was inside the largest of
the hogans propped up against the back wall. Johnny
Dinah sat by his side, but he was not bound. The
left side of the hogan was filled with grim-faced
Navajo warriors, all in buckskin. They wore their
long hair gathered and bound in back, a woven
cotton ribbon as a head band. Off to the right of
the center, the women sat on sheepskins and there
were many of them. Some wore buckskin while
others were dressed in the crude cotton dress of
their own weaving. Even while his head ached

viciously, Tom had to admit they were fine looking people. Their faces held a fierce pride that a
man could not help but respect.

And then, on the other side of him, Tom noticed
Hosteen Nez. His face was bloody and an open cut
was on his right cheek. He too had fought, and
Tom felt a queer twist of pride and of pity as he
looked at him.

"It is bad," Hosteen Nez whispered softly.

Tom turned to Johnny, whose face was sullen,
angry and baffled. "What is it, Johnny?"

"They are fools," Johnny said in English. "They
want to hear you tell them why you came."

"Shall I?"

"They won't believe you, but tell them," Johnny
said bitterly.

One of their captors said, "You say he speaks
the language of The People, Chee. We will listen."

At that moment, a girl spoke up from the
woman's side and they all turned to listen. She
was a slight girl with a coppery skin and deep
black eyes that were angry now. Her black hair
was faultlessly done, brushed back sleekly to a
knot at the back of her head. She was slim, beauti-
ful even by the white man's standards.

"He cannot speak our language," the girl said
contemptuously. "Chee said he could fight too.
He cannot. And I do not think he can speak either."

"You are wrong, Asson Tsosie," Tom said
quietly. "You are too proud."

The girl looked startled, and Tom knew that he
had guessed her identity correctly.

"In my country it is a squaw's fight when many
men conquer one man. It is not a warrior's way."
His voice was cold, sarcastic.

Johnny Dinah's wife lifted her lip in a sneer. "You have no warriors."

"Ask Hosteen Nez if we have warriors," Tom said.

They all turned to look at Tall Man.

"It is true," he said quietly. "They captured me and killed my mother. They all have firesticks which you cannot fight. There are many of them at the canyon, more than a whole clan of us. They are burning our hogans and killing our sheep and cutting our trees and destroying our seed. They are powerful, with many horses and many firesticks."

"Yet you bring this man as your slave," Slim One said.

"I am his slave," Hosteen Nez said. "Listen to his words. They are true."

They looked at Tom now.

"Tell them the truth," Johnny Dinah murmured. "Make them believe."

"Seven treaties you have made with the white man," Tom began, "and seven times you proved yourselves liars. The White Chief is patient, but not forever. His patience is at an end. He has warriors in your country now and they will destroy you. They will hunt you to the sacred mountain of the north and kill you unless you obey what they say."

"What do they say?" Slim One asked haughtily.

"You are to journey south to the white man's house and surrender yourselves. He will feed you and will give you skins, but he will not let you stay in this land. You will go to another land until you learn that The People cannot lie to the white man."

There was an angry murmuring among the men. The women seemed amused.

"And did the White Chief send you to destroy our clan?" Slim One asked finally. "Are your warriors so great that one of you can conquer us?"

"I came to warn you to surrender. Or you will be killed."

"Why should you warn us?" a man asked.

"Chee, son of Hosteen Tla, is my friend," Tom said quietly. "I came to save him from our warriors."

Slim One looked at the men and then at the woman. By silent consent, she seemed to be the spokesman for the clan.

"White man, ever since we came from the Blue House, we have lived here and fought. We have conquered the Utes and the tribes who lived in houses. They are our slaves. We have conquered the people to the south, and they are our slaves. We raid many moons away and come back conquerors. We are The People. The Gods like us and will never let us be conquered. Your tongue is false, just as Chee's tongue is false when your Gods put a spell on him. You are a son of Coyote."

Johnny Dinah said angrily. "Foolish girl! Your clan is blind! What he says is true. I have seen it!"

"A son of Coyote," Slim One repeated. "Your scalp will look well at the Yebitchai when the land is green again."

Johnny Dinah groaned.

"That is all," Slim One said. "We will feed you before we kill you. For The People are rich and can feed the dead."

It was the end of the parley. The women threw sticks on the fire that burned in the middle of the hogan and were soon about the business of preparing mutton and meal.

Tom shut his eyes and leaned his head back against the wall. It was terribly necessary to think and think straight now, but his head ached miserably.

"This girl," he said softly in English. "She is your wife, Johnny?"

"Yes," Johnny answered bitterly. "She is brave, but she is also blind."

"You would not leave her?"

Johnny was silent a moment. "Yes, to get you out of here, Tom. But I would come back to her."

"Perhaps we can take her with us," Tom suggested.

Johnny's face remained calm, for they were being watched, but there was an undertone of excitement in his voice as he asked, "How?"

"Where are the guns?"

"We must not shoot them, Tom. I cannot."

"Not them. But others, once we make our escape good."

"They are in the snow outside where they fell. My people will not touch them."

Tom studied the men in the hogan and then said, "They have no weapons, Johnny."

"They do not think you are a warrior, Tom. It is a sign of contempt."

"And a good one," Tom murmured. "They will unbind me to feed me?"

"Yes."

"I will ask to stretch my legs and rise. Then we will make a rush for the door. You go first and get horses. One for me, one for you, one for Slim One and one for Hosteen Nez if he fights free."

"But Slim One," Johnny protested. "How will we bring her?"

"You have the horses ready," Tom said grimly. "I'll attend to that."

It was the measure of Johnny Dinah's belief in Tom that he did not question him further. And Tom only wished he had half the confidence in himself that Johnny Dinah had in him. There was no way of warning Hosteen Nez of the break, since he understood only Navajo, and to speak it would give the scheme away. That meant that single-handed he must make his escape and bring Asson Tsosie with him. To leave her meant that Johnny Dinah would return, and his return would mean death at the hands of his wife's clan. Tom's lean face settled into sleepy repose as he watched the preparation of the meal. The Navajos were conversing softly and gravely among themselves.

Tom began to grow restless. He moved against the wall and lifted himself to a higher position. Suddenly, he asked in Navajo, "Do The People feed their captives before killing them?"

"You will be fed," a man said. "We have said it."

"But how am I to eat with my hands tied?"

There was a whispered conference and then the spokesman said to Hosteen Nez, "Free him."

Hosteen Nez unbound the buckskin thongs around Tom's wrists. He stretched his hands over his head and moved his fingers and then he said contemptuously to the men, "Guard the door. I am getting up to stretch." Without waiting for their permission he rose. He had to bend down a little to clear the ceiling and, indifferently, he looked over at the women, with contempt. The men had accepted his jibe about guarding the low door. They had not done so. The way was clear. Asson Tsosie was sitting in the front row of women, watching him.

Tom raised a leg and kneaded the muscles of his calf with stiff fingers. And then, before anyone suspected him, he brought his leg down in a swift kick at the fire. A shower of flaming wood and hot coals sprayed out onto the women, but Asson Tsosie, as Tom had planned, received most of the fire in her lap. There was only half-light left in the hogan as Tom lunged for the low door. But before he could achieve it, Johnny Dinah had streaked past him and out it.

There was a concert of screams from the women. Tom cleared the door, then wheeled to face it, his hands fisted. The second man out was Hosteen Nez, and he had to fight his way. The Indians had tried to stop him, and even now they had hold of his arms. Tom slugged past Hosteen Nez's head and hit a face in the dark. Tall Man came free and fell on the snow.

"Stay and take Slim One!" Tom said swiftly.

There was bedlam in the hogan now. In several places, Tom could see, fire was starting. The first person out was a man. Tom brought his fist down on the man's neck as he stooped low to pass through the door. Hosteen Nez dragged him out and threw him in the snow. Next came a fat squaw whose cotton dress was flaming. Tom let her pass. Then there was turmoil inside and from it and out the door came Slim One, her dress blazing. Tom saw Hosteen Nez grab her and throw her down into the snow, and then there was the sound of a struggle behind him. But he forgot that, for his attention now was centered on the hogan door. The warriors were struggling to get out.

Feet planted far apart for bracing, Tom fought. As soon as a head and shoulders appeared out of the door, he would slug. If they did not disappear immediately, he kicked. It was savage, bloody, brutal, but it had to be done. His fists ached from slugging Navajo skulls, and still they would not give up. A leaden weariness crept up his arms. The Indians were fighting in pure panic now, for the hogan had caught fire.

Then the first man Hosteen Nez had dragged from the doorway rose shakily from the snowbank and, sizing things up, rushed at Tom. Tom saw him and had to turn to face him to protect himself. It was the signal for the Indians to pour out of the hogan like water spilled from a jar.

Tom drove a savage left in the Navajo's face as he tried to wrestle and then turned to confront the Indians boiling toward him. It would be suicide to fight longer.

He turned and raced off towards the corrals, the Indians in pursuit. Halfway there, he saw the horses loom out of the dark. Hosteen Nez held a riderless horse. Johnny Dinah, with Asson Tsosie in front of him, was leading another riderless horse. Tom, without pausing in his stride, jumped on the nearest horse and Johnny Dinah wheeled off toward the north. The others fell in line, galloping out of camp. Behind them, the angry yells of the Navajos rose on the night air.

Soon they were on a narrow trail that followed the creek up the mountains. They rode for perhaps ten minutes when Johnny Dinah pulled up and waited for the others.

"Are you hurt?" he asked Tom.

"No. Did you get the guns?"

"They were gone," Johnny said simply. "They picked them up."

"Then we have no weapons?" Tom asked.

"None. Not even a knife."

There was a long moment of silence, which was broken by Slim One saying, "The People will kill you now, Chee."

"The People will not catch me," Johnny answered. "I drove off the horses."

"They will travel far."

"And so will we," Johnny said. "There is a horse for you. Ride it."

Slim One said calmly, "I will not."

Roughly, Johnny pushed her off his horse to the ground and then dismounted himself, facing her. "Woman," he said quietly, angrily, "you may speak well in council, but you do not act well in war. I have not yet beat you, but if you do not mount your horse and ride between me and the white friend, I will prove to you that a woman's words cannot turn a man's blow. Do you hear?"

For one astounded moment Slim One regarded Johnny, and then she said softly, "Chee. It is not well to speak to a woman so."

"It is not well to die for your pride. Now ride."

In complete submission, Asson Tsosie walked over to her horse. In the dark, Tom smiled. The Navajos, apparently, let their women rule them only so long as they chose. But soon, his thoughts turned to what Johnny had told him. Without weapons of any sort, they would have to cross a hundred miles of Navajo country. Perhaps they could bluff it, but the thought of their helplessness angered him.

Apparently, Johnny had been thinking of the

same thing, for he called them together and talked in Navajo, consulting with Hosteen Nez.

"We are helpless," he announced. "The safest way is over these mountains, following north to the white man's land and the Utes'. Perhaps then, we can dodge The People after Asson Tsosie's clan sets them against us."

This course was decided upon, then. They rode all through the long night, Johnny guiding them up the mountain trail, trying to put many miles between them and the five hogans on Red Creek. Johnny had said no word of thanks to Tom yet for risking his life to save him, but Tom understood the reticence. It was one he would have practiced himself.

Just before daybreak, they made camp in order to allow Johnny and Hosteen Nez to set buckskin rabbit snares. There was a little moonlight, but they decided to risk a fire. By daylight, it would have died to coals so the rabbits could be cooked and still not leave a sign of smoke in the air. Their luck held. By the time Johnny had set the fifth snare, there was a rabbit in the first. And when full daylight came, they had eaten well and were on the trail again. It wound up through the timber, huge pines making the forest gloomy and secretive. The snow was not so heavy in the thick timber, and the only tracks they encountered were those of the animals.

All that day they rode steadily and Asson Tsosie was quiet as death. To her, Johnny's actions were a betrayal of The People and it hurt her pride. Toward nightfall, they were approaching the top of the pass. This was as far as Asson Tsosie or Johnny had been, and, like all primitive people, they were a little awed at the thought of what they might see on the other side of the mountains. The approach, therefore, to the ridge was slow, cautious.

Johnny Dinah dismounted just before they reached the top, a point of rock swept bare of snow with only the darkening sky beyond. He climbed up to it cautiously and when he achieved the ridge, he stopped. Then he dropped on all fours and rolled down the ridge, stopping just in front of Tom.

"Utes," he said sharply, pointing over the ridge.

There were six of them, a Ute scouting party undoubtedly. They were camped on the very lip of a cliff with wickiups thrown up against the wind. On the edge of the cliff, in front of the fire, six rifles were stacked, after the fashion of the soldiers they had seen in the forts of their reservation. The picture was eloquent, telling Tom many things. In the first place, the Utes were so confident that they had camped in the most exposed place they could find. In the second place, it meant that they were on the warpath in behalf of the white man. Tom knew enough, by hearsay, of the Utes to be sure their chance of escaping were nil if they walked down into that camp and gave themselves up. As long as the Utes were under the leadership of whites, they were sullenly docile. But to find one white and three Navajos alone and unarmed in this mountain fastness would be a stroke of fortune they would not question. Scalps were prized, and white ones more highly than their traditional Navajo ones since the white man had subjected them. In such a situation, the Ute would revert back to the ways of twenty years past. The white men be damned! Besides, who would ever know what had happened in these wild mountains?

The same thoughts were running through Johnny

Dinah's head as, along with Hosteen Nez, the three of them watched the Ute camp from a screening scrub oak thicket.

Tom beckoned them down the ridge and they went back down the trail and into the forest where Asson Tsosie had been ordered to take the horses. A whicker from one of them would be disastrous. Squatting in the shelter of a windfall, Johnny told his wife what they had seen. Then he looked over at Tom.

"Tomorrow," Tom said in Navajo, "they will pick up our trail and follow it. They will kill us."

Johnny nodded. "Then they will go down our backtrail to kill The People. The men of Asson Tsosie's clan cannot fight firesticks."

Tom nodded. He and Johnny were thinking along the same unpleasant lines, he could see, but Johnny was reluctant to speak. For Johnny already knew that the Utes were the allies of the whites in this war against the Navajos. Could he ask Tom to kill his own allies?

Tom settled the question for him. "They must not be allowed to go on," he said quietly. He had solved the problem in his own mind. Johnny Dinah was his friend, and Johnny's people would be at the mercy of these murdering Utes who had no idea of justice, only murder and plunder. Better six dead Utes than forty Navajos whom they would kill in a bitterly unfair fight.

Hosteen Nez said, "But they have firesticks."

"We will surprise them," Tom said. He caught Asson Tsosie looking at him strangely, as if she could not believe her ears. Her expression said, "Is the white friend going to fight for The People?" Tom looked at Johnny.

"When they are fed and slow of thought," he

said in Navajo, "we will surprise their camp." He went on to detail the plan. Johnny and Hosteen Nez listened gravely, and at the end Hosteen Nez said, "It is bad. We will die."

Tom turned to Asson Tsosie and said mockingly, "Can you give this man of The People courage?"

Asson Tsosie flushed. "He said that it was bad. He did not say that he was afraid."

"Maybe the ears of the white man are too sharp," Tom said sardonically, looking at Hosteen Nez.

Tall Man lowered his eyes. "If you say it, I shall fight."

"I say it," Tom said bluntly.

It was cruel, Tom knew, but he needed Hosteen Nez. He also knew that Hosteen Nez was not so much afraid as he was chary of a new thing. He had never fought these Utes before, and now he was called upon to fight them when they had guns. But pity did not enter into Tom's talk. He wanted to goad Hosteen Nez into a fight which would be despearate. Johnny Dinah understood and he turned away to hide a sad smile.

At full dark, the three of them set out. They first determined the direction of the wind, then made a wide circle that would bring them close to the camp in screening timber. The Ute horses had been staked down the slope a ways. Tom chose the most dangerous role for himself, since he wanted to set an example. He was to crawl up behind the wickiup. Hosteen Nez and Johnny were to approach from downslope, the only vantage point feasible. Once Tom was ready, he was to wait long enough to make certain that the other two were ready, then they would rush the camp.

They parted in the dark and Tom gave them

time to swing down the slope and come up again.
Then he set out.

As a child, he had been schooled well enough in
Indian ways to understand the tricks of their stealth.
There was none better than the Apache school.
Soon, he could see the fire, but he did not get
down on all fours. He mastered his impatience,
knowing that an Indian would sometimes work all
night to sneak up on a camp like this.

An hour passed and he was closer, almost behind the brush wickiup. He could hear the guttural
conversation of the Utes. They were smoking;
occasionally, one of them would rise and throw
logs on the fire. Only an Indian made a fool by his
own confidence would have acted so openly in
hostile country.

Tom waited a long time there, perfectly motionless, until his feet were almost numb with cold.
When he judged that Johnny and Tall Man were in
their positions, he waited until the fire had died
again and was replenished. When it was burning
brightly, he gathered himself for the rush.

His run past the wickiup was as noiseless as he
could make it, and he headed straight beyond the
fire for the stacked rifles. He did not hear a sound
until he reached the rifles and whirled. The six
Utes were on their feet staring.

He determined to give them a chance. "I am
taking your guns," he said calmly in English,
hoping they would understand. "Sit down."

For answer, the nearest Ute raised his tomahawk
and threw it with a sidearm motion that was as
swift as it was wicked. Tom tried to dodge, but it
slammed against his shoulder with an impact that
staggered him and seemed to crush his arm.

He had been a fool! With a yell, the Utes

swarmed toward him. Johnny Dinah's whoop filled the night and he and Hosteen Nez jumped into the firelight. They each had a heavy club and Tom saw Johnny snatch a tomahawk from the Ute's belt before he realized that two of the Utes were rushing him. He tried to grab for a rifle, but his right arm was numb. Desperately then, he kicked the stacked rifles over the cliff edge, stooped and grasped the handle of the thrown tomahawk in his left hand just as the Utes were upon him.

Awkwardly, he parried a vicious downsweep of the second Ute's tomahawk and then jabbed his own in the Indian's midriff stopping his rush. The first Ute had a knife raised and Tom struck savagely at it. He saw it arc off in a glitter of steel just as the Ute screamed. The second Indian was up now, facing him, slashing expertly with the sharp end of the tomahawk. Slowly, using his own weapon as a clumsy shield, Tom backed off. The feeling was slowly coming into his right arm again. But under his feet, he felt the cliff edge, and he knew that if he were to save himself, he must act now. The second Ute was searching in the snow for his knife.

Tom parried a blow of the Ute tomahawk with the haft of his own and then kicked out viciously. He caught the Indian in the stomach and he jackknifed forward. With a short sweep of his weapon, Tom brought his weapon down on the Ute's skull. And then, before he knew it, the second Ute had dived into him, arm raised, knife flashing in the firelight.

He felt himself lose his balance. He raised his tomahawk over his head, the haft of it against the knife arm of the Ute, and with his right arm he grabbed the buckskin shirt of the Indian. Slowly, almost majestically, locked in each other's arms, they teetered over the edge.

What Tom had thought was a cliff was only a steep snow-covered slope of rocks. As he felt himself going, he twisted his body so that the Ute was under him. The Indian lit in the snow on his back and in a tangle of arms and legs and a cloud of snow they plummeted down the slope. Tom remembered to hold the tomahawk over his head, barring the knife from striking, but he could not do it for long. He felt both the arms of the Ute around him, and guessed that in the panic the Ute had dropped his knife also. Snow filled his mouth. His head rapped against a rock but he clung desperately to the Indian.

When he felt their slide slacking, he started to fight again. Holding the Indian's head in the crook of his arm, he smashed blow after blow at the face, his arms pumping savagely. The Ute's hand crawled up his face, fingers searching for his eyes. Tom bit the hand and felt warm blood in his mouth, heard the Ute's sharp cry. And now they were stopped, buried deep in a snowbank. With a sharp twist of his body, he was on top of the kicking Indian. He knew now that the Ute's knife was gone. One hand choking the Indian, then, he slugged blow after blow at the Ute's face. At the fifth one, he felt the body slack under him. But he kept on, striking with both hands now. When he was tired, he ceased, dragging in great sobs of breath. The Indian was under him, still as stone. And then Tom realized that the Ute had been pinned down to bare and jagged rock. His skull would be crushed by now.

He staggered to his feet, looking up the slope.

He could hear the sound of fighting up there. Up the slope ten feet was one of the rifles. Frantically, Tom worked his way to it, got it, and continued up, his lungs almost burst with the panting.

Almost at the top now, he fought savagely for wind. As his head rose over the edge, he took the scene in with one swift glance. Hosteen Nez was on his back, doing his mightiest to stay the arm of a huge Ute with knife in hand. Tom leveled the rifle and shot, and the Ute rolled over. Johnny Dinah, with a bloody stick of heavy firewood in his hand, was matching battle with the single Ute left standing, who was wielding a tomahawk like a wild flail. And Asson Tsosie, a stick of firewood in her hand, was harrying the Ute from behind.

Tom shot again and the Ute, as if glad to die, simply folded into the snow. The camp was not a pretty sight now. One of the Utes, a knife in his chest, lay across the fire. Another had his head laid open and was lying on his face. The two that were shot lay peacefully on their backs. The fifth lay half over the edge of the cliff. The sixth, below, Tom was glad no one could see.

Johnny Dinah grinned weakly at the sight of Tom. His bloody shirt was ribboned with knife cuts which he ignored. He reached out for Asson Tsosie and pulled her to him.

"Our women can fight," he told Tom in English. "She killed one Ute, Tom."

Hosteen Nez had a shattered hand where he had tried to stop the blow of a tomahawk. But none of them was hurt badly. None of the knife wounds were deep and with the Ute's own herbs, which she found in a buckskin sack, Asson Tsosie bandaged their wounds.

When she came to Tom, she smiled up into his eyes. "I believe you now," she said simply. "The white friend is a true warrior."

It was at noon next day that they sighted the band of Carson's volunteers which had set out from Defiance ahead of Tom. The snow on the flats was not deep now, only a slush. Tom and the other three were sighted almost as soon as they pulled out of the timber and the volunteers stopped to wait for them.

Approaching, Tom could see they were mostly Mexicans, about seventy of them. Their captain was an American, a trapper from the Ute country.

He greeted Tom with warmth and then looked at the others.

"Fight, huh?" he observed.

And Tom, who had fought what his own people would have called a friendly ally, looked over at Johnny Dinah and his wife and at Hosteen Nez. Blind and proud and fierce as the Navajo people were, if they could produce three such as this, they were worth saving. He turned to the officer and lied. He did it blandly, with feeling, knowing he was right.

"Yes," he said calmly. "These are friendly Navajos on their way to surrender. Their clan wouldn't let them go. We had a mighty tough fight to get away."

"Looks it," the trapper said, nodding his head sympathetically. "Did you see anything of my Ute scouts when you were up that way?"

"Nothing," Tom lied. "But if they're headed over the mountains, they're as good as dead."

"They've got guns," the trapper said, surprise in his voice.

"So have the Navajos," Tom said again. "There are two hundred of them there in the mountains. Unless you want to commit suicide, I wouldn't take the men up.".

The trapper shook his head immediately. "Don't worry," he said quietly. "This murderin' sticks in my craw. I'll sashay to the south, cover a piece of country, kill a few sheep and wait for 'em to starve out. I've got a bellyfull of murderin' people I like."

Tom got food from them and then the four of them set out for the south. Next day, in the middle of a vast brown plain, Tom pulled up and pointed to far distant mountains to the east. "Over there in Santa Fe, Johnny. That's my way." He pointed south. "That is your way."

Johnny nodded gravely and spoke in Navajo. "What will happen to our people, Tom? What will happen to us?"

Tom only shook his head. "Whatever it is, Johnny, see it through. Over east our people are at war and I must help them. Later, when it is over, I will come back and help you."

Asson Tsosie pulled her horse up beside Tom's. "Chee's white friend is my white friend," she said simply. "If we must be punished for our pride, let it be."

And that was the parting, Hosteen Nez and Johnny Dinah and Asson Tsosie heading toward the white man's fort and exile, and Tom heading back for the war. But if, Tom thought soberly as he watched them ride off, in the midst of all this killing those three were to come through, all was not so bad.

He pulled his horse around and headed east.